BRAHMAPUTRA

Celebrating
30 Years of Publishing
in India

BRAHMAPUTRA

BRAHMAPUTRA

The Ahom Son Rises – 1

Vijayendra Prasad

with Kulpreet Yadav

HarperCollins *Publishers* India

First published in India by HarperCollins *Publishers* in 2023
4th Floor, Tower A, Building No. 10, DLF Cyber City,
DLF Phase II, Gurugram, Haryana – 122002
www.harpercollins.co.in

2 4 6 8 10 9 7 5 3 1

P-ISBN: 978-93-5699-052-4
E-ISBN: 978-93-5699-051-7

Typeset in 11/14.7 Minion Pro at
Manipal Technologies Ltd, Manipal

Printed and bound at
Thomson Press (India) Ltd

This book is dedicated to the brave Ahom people whose courage and sacrifice stopped the expansion of the Mughals in the east.

CHAPTER 1

Jorhat, Ahom capital, Assam, 1664

Swargadeo Jayadhwaj Singha, the twenty-first heavenly king of the Ahom kingdom, had been speaking non-stop for two hours. 'From the time I became the king of the mighty Ahom empire, I have added more territories. The Ahoms are the mightiest now and I, as your god, am alone responsible for bringing this moment of glory into your lives. If anyone dares to look in our direction, I will lead our army on an elephant and crush them. Have you ever heard of a braver king?'

The king was short, around five feet three, and the most noticeable feature on his face were his eyes, which were large and unblinking. He was seated on his golden throne that was encrusted with precious stones. His rotund body was wrapped in silk, a ceremonial gamosa was loosely tied on his waist as a tongali and a silk safa rested on his head.

Behind the king stood a dozen armed guards. The members of his court were seated facing him with an aisle that separated them.

With a distinct sparkle in his eyes, the king looked at their faces one by one, as he waited for an answer, but the leaders of the state stared back at him, unmoving and expressionless.

The king flicked his head towards his left. A servant in cotton clothes, who was holding an ornamental jug, immediately approached him. Without looking in his direction, Jayadhwaj extended his hand, which held a glass tumbler. The servant filled it with luk-lao, rice wine. He brought the glass close to his lips and took a large gulp. Because of the effort of speaking continuously, his face now had a sheen of sweat.

Seated on his right was Borphukan, the military commander, a tall, well-built man who wore a suti sula and suria. The muscles on Borphukan's neck were taut and his skin sun-tanned. His hair was short and he wore the scars on his body as battle trophies. His eyes were devoid of any emotion.

Next to Borphukan was his pregnant wife, Yashodhara, an elegant and beautiful woman in a mekhela and chador. With her large eyes, plump lips and straight jet-black hair, she had a magnetic charm that made it difficult for anyone to keep their eyes off her. She was so well-known for her sharp mind and strategic thinking that the king himself invited her to the court for special meetings. Now, she turned her head to look at her husband, but his eyes were on his master.

On Borphukan's other side were the two Dangarias, Buragohain and Borgohain, who were minor rulers under Jayadhwaj. Identically dressed, their ornaments and the quality of silk used for their clothes were indicators that, except the king, everyone else was below them in Ahom hierarchy. While Buragohain was tall and obese, resembling a sumo wrestler, Borgohain was a thin man of medium height. Both sported sparse moustaches but had no beards.

On Jayadhwaj's left were the patra mantris, the five council ministers of the Ahom kingdom. The oldest among them was the prime minister, Himabhas, a tall man of average build whose face had a permanent smile. Being the chief servant of the king for a long time, and as someone who took care of all administrative affairs of the state, his back was slightly bent forward as if he was forever seeking the approval of the king.

At the end of this group, farthest from the king, sat a Shaiva sadhu. He was a short, slender man with beady eyes and a sparse grey moustache that merged with his equally meagre beard like a thin waterfall. His torso was bare and a cotton suria was draped around his legs. Ash was smeared all over his body and a rudraksha garland hung from his neck. On his forehead were three horizontal lines of ash with a red mark at the centre. The sadhu was staring at the king, visibly angry.

Jayadhwaj resumed his self-congratulatory monologue, 'I know none of you will say anything. Ask me how I know!' He paused briefly before continuing, 'That's because you have nothing to say. Swargadeo Jayadhwaj Singha is the bravest king on the earth, and no one can defeat him!' He broke into laughter.

The sadhu couldn't take it any longer. He jumped to his feet.

All heads turned to look at him, uncertain about what would happen next.

The sadhu began to speak, 'Swargadeo Jayadhwaj, this much ego and pride is not good. I have been listening to you since morning. All you have done is praise yourself. Let me remove the veil of obsession from your eyes. The truth is, you have not achieved all this by yourself. What about our gods? What about our ancestors' blessings? What about our powerful army and the navy? You think you could have achieved all this without their blessings and support?'

Jayadhwaj's laughter turned hysterical. After pausing for a few seconds, he said, 'Sadhu maharaj, I don't want to disrespect you. But whatever I have told you is the truth. Everyone knows that without *my* leadership, *my* intelligence and *my* courage, we wouldn't have achieved anything.' Every time he uttered the word "my", he raised his voice several notches higher, simultaneously hitting his chest with a closed fist.

The sadhu looked towards his left and then his right. Clearly, he hadn't expected a response like this from the Swargadeo of the Ahom kingdom. Now, he looked angrier. The sadhu took two steps forward. He was now standing in the aisle facing Jayadhwaj.

Worried about the king's safety, a dozen sentries rushed towards him. Jayadhwaj raised his hand, and they stopped midway and returned to their positions.

'You are our guest, sadhu maharaj, so you are free to say anything. You may not respect the Ahom Swargadeo but the Ahom Swargadeo respects you. Speak freely!'

With his nostrils flared, eyes narrowed and forehead creased, the sadhu said, 'Swargadeo Jayadhwaj, because of your ego, the Ahom kingdom's flag will be defeated very soon!'

His declaration was met with a shocked silence. The air stood still. The members of the court exchanged nervous glances with each other.

Finally, Jayadhwaj brought his glass to his lips. It was empty. His servant rushed forward to refill it, but Jayadhwaj flung the glass away. It fell on the ground, clanging loudly.

Jayadhwaj asked, 'When?'

The sadhu replied, 'When the hair on your head turns grey.'

Everyone's eyes widened in horror. Only Yashodhara had a faint smile on her face.

Jayadhwaj stood up, looking uncertain. Then, after mumbling his thanks to everyone, he abruptly left the court.

———•———

Borphukan and Yashodhara entered the gates of their palace. Though large and well-guarded, it was only a quarter of the size of Jayadhwaj's palace.

By the time they walked inside, Yashodhara had started to complain of pain in her abdomen. Borphukan lovingly supported her till they reached their private chambers.

As servants attended to Yashodara, Borphukan walked across to the terrace. He looked at the grasslands around the palace. In the distance, he could see blue hills and a portion of the Brahmaputra that was caressing the foothills as it made its way westwards across the Ahom kingdom.

The August sun was about to set. The air was warm and humid. Borphukan wiped the sweat off his face and the exposed parts of his body with a silk gamosa. A servant brought him a glass of luk-lao. He sipped the liquid gratefully, inhaled deeply and sat down in an elaborate bamboo chair under the shade of an umbrella made of bamboo leaves. His deep-set eyes were distant, and his taut jawline showed the worry the day's proceedings had wreaked in him.

Later, in his bed, as the commander of the Ahom army lay beside his wife, he looked at her and asked, 'How are you feeling now, Yashodhara?'

She smiled tenderly but complained, 'Your son is troubling me.'

It was his turn to smile as he said, 'You think it is time?'

She shook her head. 'It will take another week, I have been told.' After a pause, she asked, 'Are you worried about what the sadhu said today?'

Borphukan nodded. Then he closed his eyes.

Yashodhara waited for a few seconds for him to add something, but when he didn't, she closed her eyes too.

Within minutes, as she drifted into sleep, she saw a stunning image. In her dream, a large army was approaching the gates of the Ahom capital. Surrounded by his military commanders, the patra mantris, and both the Gohains, Jayadhwaj looked pale and frightened.

That's when a young man approached Yashodhara and touched her feet. He was a tall and well-built man in metal body armour and a metal helmet. In his hand, he held a hengdang sword, the largest she had seen in her life. At that moment, her face was reflected in its blade. She frowned. In the reflection, she looked much older. Who's this young man, she wondered.

The young man said, 'Mother, bless your son, so that he can protect the Ahom kingdom.'

Yashodhara had tears in her eyes. She swallowed hard as she whispered, 'I bless you, my son. I bless you, my Lachit.'

With that, Yashodhara woke up, sweating and breathless. It took a few seconds for her breathing to stabilize and for her to realize she was in her own room. She placed her hand on her abdomen and felt the kicks of her unborn child. She relaxed.

Her movements woke up Borphukan too, and he looked at his wife, worried.

She spoke before he did. 'I saw our son. He was about to leave to face the enemy. And he sought my blessing.'

'What are you talking about, Yashodhara?'

She looked at him and blinked, 'Our son, Lachit. I saw Lachit Borphukan.'

He seemed irritated and closed his eyes again, 'Sleep, sweetheart. Our son is yet to be born.'

'No, no, wait ... I have to go now to the Mahadeo temple across the river to seek his blessings.'

Without opening his eyes, Borphukan whispered, 'Don't be a child, Yashodhara. You are in no condition to cross the river. We will go tomorrow morning.'

'But I have to go *now*. I *have* to pray at Lord Shiva's temple.'

In response, she heard the low snores of her husband. He had dozed off while she was still talking to him. She sighed.

After a few moments, she stepped down from the bed, changed her clothes, covered her head and left the palace. The guard at the gate opened his mouth to say something, but she stopped him with a gesture.

Fifteen minutes later, when she reached the banks of the Brahmaputra, she was sweating due to the effort. It was dark, but because the moon was in three quarters and there weren't many clouds in the sky, the river and the outlines of the surrounding area were visible. She looked in all directions.

Finally, she spotted what her eyes were searching for. She approached a tree that was right on the edge of the bank of the river. As she neared, the sounds of the moving water grew louder. She reached for the rope that was tied to the tree and opened the knot. As one end of the rope was free, she pulled the rope towards herself, and a small boat came into view. With a smile on her face, she took a step towards the boat.

But, as she felt her unborn child move inside her, she stopped. She appeared to be in a lot of pain but dragged herself forward once again, her mind visualizing the Shiva temple on the opposite bank. She closed her eyes. She could even hear the temple bells and the drum beats of the damaru, Lord Shiva's favourite musical instrument.

As her pain subsided, she opened her eyes again and stepped into the boat. It wobbled under her weight but stabilized as she sat down in it. Then, her lips mumbling a silent prayer, she began to row towards the opposite bank.

As the boat moved into deeper waters, it started to rain. This was not good. Within a few minutes, the waves turned higher. She stopped midstream and clutched the gunwales tightly on both sides as the boat rocked treacherously. She looked around, now worried. That's when she realized she was going into labour. The oars fell into the water and drifted away. Now, she was at the mercy of nature.

She turned and saw a huge wave approaching the boat. Terrified, she took a deep breath. All she could do was stare at the dark wall of water coming towards her. The wave lifted the boat and then slipped away. For a fraction of a second, Yashodhara's boat hung in the air and then it fell on the water with a loud crash. The hull of the boat jarred deafeningly. Yashodhara's grip on the gunwales loosened and her face hit the boat. She cried in pain and looked around again. That's when she saw the next wave. Another wall of water was heading towards the boat. In the next second, the wave consumed the boat, and as it hurled it forward, the churn in the water capsized the boat.

Yashodhara's vision blurred as water entered her eyes. The pain in her abdomen increased. She moved her legs and hands frantically and felt her body lift through the water.

Moments later, her face was above the water, but she was struggling to stay afloat. That's when she felt her baby take birth underwater. By now, Yashodhara was only partly conscious, though her lips were mumbling a prayer.

After the baby was delivered in the water, due to the smell of the blood from the delivery, a crocodile found its way. The crocodile affectionately cut the umbilical cord with its scales, separating the baby from the mother. The crocodile then whispered to the baby, 'Chhota bhai, you are Brahmaputra's son now and we crocodiles are your family. We will always protect you.'

Meanwhile, spent, the mother pulled the umbilical cord but found no baby at its end. Her lips stopped mumbling the prayer and her eyes widened with terror as she saw many crocodiles were circling around her. Was this the end?

That's when she spotted her tiny son flapping his feet and moving towards her even though his eyes were still closed.

She grabbed her baby. The crocodiles kept their distance. Relieved, she whispered as she kissed her child, 'Lachit, my son—you will be the bravest.'

CHAPTER 2

Five years later

On a late afternoon in June, Borphukan, the commander-in-chief of the Ahom army, walked into his palace. There was mud and blood all over him, but the smile on his face was the widest that anyone had seen in a long time. In one hand he held his naked hengdang, its blade smeared with blood, and in the other, his helmet. His walk was relaxed and his head was held high. This was a general returning home after a decisive victory.

He was followed by ten paiks, or soldiers. Outside the palace, around fifty more paiks were holding off hundreds of his countrymen with bamboo barricades. These men were jostling at the periphery of the palace grounds, shouting slogans of victory, trying to catch a glimpse of their national hero.

Their slogans echoed in the palace, 'Victory to Ahoms, victory to Ahoms!' followed by 'Borphukan ki jai! Swargadeo Jayadhwaj ki jai!'

Inside the palace, Yashodhara rushed towards her husband with a plate that had earthen lamps arranged on it along with a Kopou ful, or foxtail orchid. Following her was their five-year-old son, Lachit, and several attendants.

She stopped two feet from Borphukan and started a prayer. Her eyes were closed and her hands moved in a circle. A minute later, she opened her eyes, and her smile matched that of her husband's. She took another step towards him, picked a sweet from the plate and extended her hand. The General opened his mouth to accept the prasad. Yashodhara had tears in her eyes; these were the tears of happiness.

Borphukan looked down at his son who was hiding behind his mother's legs. He bent down and scooped him up. As he held him in his arms and kissed him, the little boy didn't protest.

Yashodhara said, 'Careful … all the blood on you will scare him.'

Borphukan raised his head to look at her and said, 'He is Borphukan's son. His karma is to kill enemies of the Ahom state.' Then he looked down at his son once again, smiled and asked, 'Son, are you scared?'

The little boy pulled out a small wooden hengdang that he was hiding behind him all this while and raised his hand to challenge his father.

Borphukan laughed and said, 'Didn't I tell you, Yashodhara? Didn't I tell you that our son will be the next Borphukan of the Ahom army?'

In his sweet and feminine voice, Lachit shouted, 'Victory to the Ahoms, victory to Swargadeo Jayadhwaj!'

Borphukan hugged him tight. Then he pulled Yashodhara in an embrace too.

Later, a clean-looking Borphukan was eating food with his wife and son. The servants were attending to them. There were eggs, fish, chicken, vegetables and rice on the low table around which they sat with their legs folded on the carpeted floor. Fruits like litchi, mango, banana, plum and pineapple were arranged around them. Borphukan and Yashodhara were relaxed, drinking luk-lao.

In between mouthfuls of food, Borphukan said, 'Lachit has to go to gurukul soon.'

She looked up sharply. 'No, no. He's too young.'

'I didn't mean now, but eventually, we will have to let him go.'

She affectionately gazed at their son and whispered, her eyes distant but her voice steady, 'I know the battlefield is our son's destiny, Borphukan. I had seen it in my dream the day he was born.'

'Battlefield is our karmabhumi, Yashodhara, and we must prepare our son for it.'

She nodded.

Lachit looked at his mother and father, smiled and shouted again, 'Victory to the Ahoms, victory to Swargadeo Jayadhwaj!'

———·———

Seven years later

Lachit Borphukan, now twelve years old, was swimming in the Brahmaputra with other boys of his age. They were having a race when one of the boys shouted, 'Watch out, crocodile!'

All the boys stopped midstream and began to swim towards the shore, screaming, 'Help, help! Crocodile!'

But Lachit continued towards the finish line. When the boys had safely reached the shore, one of them commented, 'Why the crocodiles don't ever attack Lachit is a mystery to me.'

Another boy quipped, 'I had once asked my parents.'

'And what did they say?'

'They said crocodiles don't attack every time. They only attack when they are hungry.'

'That's precisely the mystery. How is it that whenever Lachit is in the water, their stomachs are full and they don't want to attack?'

Meanwhile, Lachit had reached the finishing point. He exulted his win before he turned to look at the shore. After an initial hesitation, his friends started to clap for him.

Lachit swam to them. When he stepped out of the river, he said, 'Look, let's cancel the results of this race. I know you got scared of the crocodile and had to abandon it.'

One of them replied, 'But Lachit, why don't you get scared of the crocodiles?'

'Should I tell you the truth?'

Everyone nodded.

'The fact is, I have no idea. My mother said I was born in the river as her boat had capsized when she was on her way to Mahadev's temple.'

One of them commented, 'You were born in a river and you didn't sink? No wonder you are such a good swimmer.'

'I feel very natural in water, friends. Even more than how I feel on land. Hmm … I'm not sure why but I feel the crocodiles seem to talk to me as if they are my pets.'

'Pets? You mean like pet dogs, pet horses, pet elephants?'

'Yes, something like that.'

He didn't reveal that the crocodiles called him 'chhota bhai' while he called them 'bada bhai'.

When Lachit returned to his palace, it was almost midday. He was surprised to see his father at home. *What was he doing here*, wondered Lachit. He should have been in the Swargadeo's court, which he knew was in session at that moment.

Next to his father sat an old man. The old man had grey eyes, a flowing full white beard and long white hair which he had tied in a bun on top of his head. His mother entered the hall just then and smiled at Lachit. But she had tears in her eyes. *What was all this about*, Lachit wondered.

Lachit looked at his mother and then at his father. His father patted the seat on a chair next to him. Lachit walked ahead to sit on it. But before he sat, he bowed down to greet the old man, 'Namaste.'

The old man smiled genially and replied, 'Namaste, Lachit.'

That's when Borphukan took a deep breath, looked at Lachit and said, 'My son, Lachit Borphukan, your time has come to leave for the gurukul.'

Yashodhara, who was still standing at an uncomfortable distance from them, gasped and covered her mouth with the end of her saree. No one looked in her direction.

The old man started to speak, 'Son, my name is Guru Jeevan Jyoti Kha. I'll be your guru at the gurukul. Your father says you are ready for your education and training. But I want to ask you, are you ready?'

Young Lachit got up and touched the old man's feet. Then he said, 'Guruji, I'm ready. I want to train to be as brave as my father.'

The old man placed his hand on young Lachit's head as a blessing. Borphukan smiled gratefully at this. He turned to look at Yashodhara, who, though she had tears in her eyes, was smiling and nodding too.

An hour later, Lachit was given an emotional send-off by Borphukan, Yashodhara and the palace guards and attendants. They watched him leave, walking alongside the Guru. When he was around fifty feet from them, he turned and smiled. That's when Yashodhara rushed forward but

Borphukan caught her hand to stop her. Lachit turned and resumed walking. Within minutes, the Guru and the young shishya disappeared in the green maze of grasslands and paddy fields.

After a day's journey on foot and on mules, the Guru and Lachit arrived at the gurukul. It was located in the middle of a jungle on the banks of the Brahmaputra River with the Himalayas right behind it.

The gurukul was a large ashram with bamboo dormitories for the shishyas, classrooms with thatched roofs, open-air akharas, two wells, a dairy farm with a dozen cows and buffaloes, a freshwater fish pond, a library hall, an amphitheatre and, on a raised hillock in the middle, the Guru's quarters made of bamboo, coconut and palm leaves. Adjacent to the ashram was an archery and spear-throwing range that was riddled with natural obstacles like rocks, rivulets, thorny bushes and marshy stretches of land.

As Lachit was being escorted to his dormitory through the ashram's pebbled walkways, he watched children his age move around. Everyone paused to acknowledge and wish the Guru but they ignored Lachit's presence.

Finally, the Guru pushed open the wooden doors of a dormitory and said, 'This is where you will live, Lachit. Here, you will not be the Borphukan's son but will be equal to all the other princes.'

'Yes, Guruji.'

Lachit looked around the hall. There were four sets of bedding rolled up against the side of the walls. Guruji pointed to one of them.

Lachit placed his bag next to the bedding and sat on it. By the time he turned around, Guruji was gone.

At that moment, an arrow came out of nowhere, missed his nose by a millimetre and struck his bag.

He jumped up and was face to face with a young boy like him. The boy laughed and said, 'I could have taken your nose today, but I didn't because you are new here.'

Lachit smiled nervously at him. The boy continued, 'My name is Chakradhwaj. I'm the crown prince of Naigaon. You?'

'My name is Lachit. I'm Borphukan's son.'

He raised his eyebrows, 'Wow! Borphukan's son?'

Lachit smiled.

'So, what are you good at? Besides not being good at saving yourself from a stranger in a new place?' Chakradhwaj winked.

'I'm here to learn. All I have done till now is swimming.'

Chakradhwaj sized him up and down. Just then, more shishyas entered the dormitory, and Chakradhwaj introduced Lachit to everyone as Borphukan's son, which seemed to impress everyone.

A few weeks later, all the students were meditating under a large banyan tree next to the Brahmaputra. They sat a few feet from one another with their legs folded and their eyes closed. There was no sign of Guruji. A gentle breeze was flowing from the north, and the surface of the Brahmaputra was unruffled.

It was six in the morning, too bright for a September dawn but tranquil nonetheless. Had a visitor crossed the spot at that time, the stillness would have made him question whether what he was watching was real or a painting.

And if the visitor decided to stay and watch closer, he would have spotted a giant python move stealthily along one of the roots hanging from the tree. Right underneath this root sat Chakradhwaj. The python was perfectly camouflaged and moving slowly without making any sound. With every passing second, it was getting closer and closer to Chakradhwaj's head.

From the edge of the river emerged a crocodile. As the python was slithering down from the root, the crocodile started to move along the mud towards the students.

A sudden gust of wind made the leaves of the tree dance and rustle for a few seconds. But the wind became gentle once again. Lachit was seated closest to the river. As he meditated, there was a calmness on his face.

The python had by now reached the tip of the hanging root. Its mouth was partially open, the movement of the forked tongue in and out of its mouth faster than before, and its eyes on Chakradhwaj. The meditating students, of course, didn't have any idea what was about to happen next.

Meanwhile, the crocodile had moved forward. It stopped just a couple of feet from Lachit.

The python continued to lower itself further, its tail tightly rolled up at the top of the root to support its weight.

As the crocodile turned its body, its tail brushed Lachit's folded legs. His eyes popped open.

Lachit looked at the crocodile, but the reptile was looking elsewhere. Alarmed, Lachit picked up his bow and arrow which was kept right next to him and turned to look in the direction of the crocodile's gaze.

The python was now inches away from Chakradhwaj, its mouth opened large enough to suck in its victim.

Lachit pulled the string and released the arrow. In a fraction of a second, the arrow entered through one side of the python's head and emerged from the other. Its grip on the root loosened and it fell on top of Chakradhwaj, who opened his eyes and jumped to his feet. The python was wriggling next to him in pain.

By now, the crocodile had returned to the water. As Chakradhwaj turned to look at Lachit, it was clear to him what had just happened. Lachit had saved his life. He embraced him, saying, 'Thank you, my friend. I will always remember this.'

'You are welcome, Prince Chakradhwaj. And as you can see, unlike you, I don't miss my target.'

Chakradhwaj laughed at the joke. Everyone else, who were on their feet by now, joined in.

------·------

Six years later

Over the years, Lachit excelled in all kinds of training and won most of the competitions. Whenever he lost, it was only to Chakradhwaj. But, in swimming and kayaking, there was no match for him. Even in boat racing, the team he led always won the race.

Lachit and Chakradhwaj were both eighteen years old now. While Lachit was six feet tall, athletic and kept his hair close-cropped like his father, Chakradhwaj was six feet two, muscular, and kept his hair long and flowing. Both their shoulders had broadened and jaws squared, and they now had a beard and moustache on their faces. If deep-felt emotions defined Lachit's actions, instinctive decisions defined Chakradhwaj's. While both best friends were ambitious, their approaches were different.

One day, Guruji summoned Lachit. Once at the door of his master's quarters, he was escorted inside by Guruji's personal assistant. Lachit was taken to the room at the end of the house where Guruji sat, his eyes closed and legs folded. There was no deity in front of the Guru, but the room was filled with incense smoke. This was the first time that Lachit had entered this room and he was surprised by its simplicity. There was no bed, no chairs or tables, only books written on sewed barks of the sanchi tree stacked up against the walls.

'This is where I live. This is all I need.' Guruji opened his eyes, smiled and continued, 'This is all *we* need.'

Lachit bowed and said, 'Yes, Guruji.'

'But to live in peace is not easy. Our enemies will not let us live in peace. Therefore, we need warriors like you. We need you to fight for our inner and outer peace.'

He bowed again.

Guruji got to his feet with agility. No one in the ashram had any idea of his exact age. He could be anywhere from sixty to a hundred years, maybe even older.

'Follow me,' he said.

Guruji led him outside the quarters and through the winding cobbled walkways until they crossed the ashram's gates. After a few minutes, they reached the Brahmaputra.

Guruji turned and said, 'Lachit, call the crocodiles.'

'What?'

'Don't act surprised. I'm your guru, your teacher. I know everything.'

'But, Guruji, I have never called them in my life. I just whisper sometimes and call them bada bhai. I think they call me chhota bhai, though their sounds are so different that I could be imagining it all.'

'No, you are not. Call them. It's an order.'

Lachit looked around at the peaceful river. The wind was gentle and the blue mountains as formidable as ever.

There was no sight of a human or an animal around them. He focused on the river but couldn't see the crocodiles.

Inhaling deeply, he shouted, 'Bada bhai! Bada bhai!'

For a few seconds nothing happened, then the placid water started to ruffle, and several eyes appeared on the surface like bubbles refusing to burst. A few moments later, the heads of the crocodiles lifted and around a dozen of them started to swim towards land. Lachit was speechless, his brows raised in surprise at the miracle unfolding before his eyes.

The crocodiles emerged out of the river, slithered a short distance on the muddy bank and stopped in front of Guruji and Lachit.

Lachit took a step forward and bent down to caress their heads one by one. He was treating them like his pets, and they were quiet as if they were in the company of their master.

Guruji turned and started to walk away. Lachit ran after him, 'Guruji, wait!'

After a hundred metres, he caught up with the Guru and spoke, out of breath, 'Guruji, they came out. But I had no idea that they would.'

Guruji stopped and turned to look at him. Then he said, 'You are a warrior of the water, son.'

'What does this mean, Guruji?'

'Well, it means what it means. If you fight your enemies over water, you would be victorious. Just like you have a real mother, Yashodhara, back at the capital, the river is your mother at battle, and the crocodiles are your subsurface paiks, your underwater soldiers.'

Lachit frowned and a shadow of worry crossed his face, 'Guruji, but I want to become a worthy borphukan like my father. I want to engage the enemy on the land and in the mountains.'

Guruji smiled. 'You will become a borphukan, my son. You are worthy of that. But you will also be the naubaicha phukan, the admiral of the Ahom's fleet. Remember, your enemy will not come from mountains in the future. Your enemies will come through the waters from the West. And you, as Lachit Borphukan and Lachit Naubaicha Phukan, will have to protect our land from them.'

With that, Guruji folded his hands towards the river and closed his eyes. Lachit did the same.

When he opened his eyes, the Guru was gone once again. Lachit walked back to the river, climbed a tree on its bank and jumped into the water. Then, for a long time, he swam in the river, the crocodiles keeping him company from all sides.

Guruji watched him from behind a tree. His face was calm as he smiled, turned and left.

———•———

The next day, all the shishyas had assembled in the amphitheatre. Guruji stood at the centre. The strong westerly wind couldn't move the braid that rested on his back but managed to stir his beard. His grey eyes seemed greyer today, and his posture suggested that he was about to embark on a solemn lecture.

Lachit was seated beside Chakradhwaj. They exchanged glances as the Guru spoke in a voice that seemed like a copy of his own voice.

'Listen, princes and Lachit, the son of the most royal officer of the mighty Ahom empire. You are the future of our race, the future of our children and the future of our peace and prosperity. Victory to Ahom!'

Everyone shouted, 'Victory to Ahom!'

'Our god, Kamakhya Devi, is our protector. But can she protect us if we are weak?'

'No,' everyone responded in chorus.

'That's right. Each one of you has done well in your training. Now, the time has come for the final competition that will prove who is the strongest.'

Everyone was listening with rapt attention.

Guruji continued, 'Tomorrow morning, you will leave for the capital of Jorhat, where a competition has been organized. Whoever wins this competition will be garlanded by the king's daughter, Padmini.'

Chakradhwaj looked at Lachit and winked. Lachit winked back. The rest looked at one another. Everyone knew what this meant. The winner would, over time, become the first in line to be considered for the role of Padmini's groom.

'Best of luck, young men. After this competition, all of you can go to your homes from Jorhat,' he paused, before continuing, 'but you must rest now. We will leave the ashram early tomorrow morning.'

Guruji left, and everyone got to their feet and bowed with folded hands in respect. Then, they dispersed.

Lachit and Chakradhwaj were now walking side by side.

Chakradhwaj asked, 'So, excited about tomorrow?'

Lachit nodded as his friend continued, 'I have heard Padmini is very beautiful.'

Lachit nodded again.

'Will you defeat me for Padmini, Lachit?'

Lachit stopped. He looked a little irritated as he spoke, 'Padmini means nothing to me. She is blue-blooded like you and the other princes. I'm the son of Borphukan, son of a royal officer. Even if I win and she garlands me, she will eventually marry one of you only.'

'Oye, oye, don't get annoyed, my friend. Royal officers can become blue-blooded too if the king decides to marry off his daughter to one of them.'

'Well, I will let you win, my friend. So that you can have her.'

Chakradhwaj raised his eyebrows, 'Let me win? It was I who has been letting you win all these years. But not tomorrow.' He laughed.

CHAPTER 3

***

Jorhat, 1682

Hundreds of people from the capital of Jorhat and nearby areas had descended to the Rang Ghar, the sports stadium where the competition of the gurukul's students was to be held. The sky was clear and the sun at ten in the morning was bright but not too hot.

The rules of the competition had been explained to the students. Each of them had been given a bow and a dozen arrows. One by one, the competitors would be asked to take their position at the centre of the arena. After this, a wild buffalo would be released. As the buffalo charged at the competitor, pigeons would be released from cages into the sky. The job of the competitor was to kill as many pigeons as possible using his bow and arrows while protecting himself from the enraged buffalo.

The open-air stadium was an annexe to the king's royal palace and connected to it through a walled passage in addition to an underground tunnel. Circular in shape with steps for seating, one side of the rang ghar's arena was covered and reserved for the members of the royal family and noblemen belonging to the top of the Ahom hierarchy. The floor of this area was layered with the finest carpets. Right in its centre was the king's throne covered in the finest of silk and, on either side, were smaller but equally elegant chairs for the king's consorts and the members of his court.

The central play area of the Rang Ghar was covered in grass, where all the competitors, including Chakradhwaj and Lachit, had assembled, visible to everyone and ready for the challenge. From where he stood, Lachit spotted his mother and father seated in the king's section. He bowed in their direction and they raised their hands in blessing.

The stadium was packed to capacity. All the members of the king's court were already seated in the royal section. All were now waiting for Swargadeo Jayadhwaj to arrive.

A man in ceremonial headgear sounded a high note using a pepa. This was followed by a group of drummers beginning to work up a rhythm, which got louder and louder with every passing second. It was a signal that the king was on his way.

A few moments later, all present got to their feet as they saw Swargadeo Jayadhwaj Singha arrive with his daughter, Padmini. The king took his throne and Padmini sat in the royal chair next to him. The king was wearing a white-coloured suti sula on his upper body, a suria on his lower body and a tongali tied on his waist, all made of silk. A silk safa rested on his head. Padmini wore an elegant off-white silk mekhla chador that had pink flowers embroidered all over it. Her round face was enveloped by dark hair that hung loose on both sides; her skin was whiter than milk, and her almond-shaped eyes were deep and mysterious.

One would have expected the princess to be dominating in her appearance and body language, with the intense gaze of authority that all powerful people are seemingly born with, but she was different. As her head moved around the stadium, Padmini looked delicate, like someone who was struggling to ride out her shaky confidence. And yet, with high cheekbones, a perfectly round chin and full lips, she clearly was—

Beautiful.

The king raised his hand and the drums stopped suddenly. The crowd roared.

Chakradhwaj's eyes were on Padmini and he was smiling ear to ear. But she was not looking at him. He followed her line of vision and realized that her eyes were on Lachit.

As Padmini's eyes met Lachit's, Lachit's face froze. He was mesmerized by her beauty and his mind stopped working. Instinctively, he raised his hand to wave at her. She noticed his gesture and smiled. Lachit abruptly brought his hand down and turned to look at Chakradhwaj, who was staring at him.

'She is … she is …' Lachit hesitated.

'You like her, don't you?'

When he spoke next, it was as if he was talking to himself, 'It seems to me that all my life, everything that I have done, Chakradhwaj, was for this moment. It's as if I knew this moment would come.'

Chakradhwaj turned to look at Padmini once again. His expression was unreadable.

The drummers started to beat the drums, but this time their rhythm was different. The crowd clapped and cheered. It was a signal that the competition was about to begin.

The students were escorted away and made to sit on the lowest steps in the arena, which were reserved for them. One by one, they would be escorted to the centre.

The name of the first candidate was announced. He was a young prince by the name of Vishnudhwaj.

There was a pin-drop silence now. To avoid the Standing in the centre of the arena, Vishnudwaj focused on the metal barrier which held the wild buffalo behind it. He already had one arrow nocked on the string of his bow in preparation.

With a loud clanking noise, the metal gate was lifted by four stout guards. For a few seconds, nothing happened. Then, a buffalo walked out. It had been hurt badly and blood trickled and dripped from its body. It was dazed for a few seconds as it looked around. Then, its eyes caught sight of its target—the young prince.

The buffalo bent its head. Its horns were now parallel to the ground. As its breathing got deeper and faster, the buffalo's nose flared, and puffs of dust started to lift in spots below its head. That's when the gate of a birdcage was opened, and a dozen pigeons fluttered out and rose in the sky.

Vishnudhwaj's eyes shot up. This was his moment. As he noticed the buffalo charge towards him from the corner of his eye, he changed the direction of his bow, pulled the string and took his first shot. Vishnudhwaj's first arrow pierced the body of a pigeon and it fell down to the ground. The next second, the flapping pigeon was crushed by the hoof of the approaching buffalo.

As Vishnudhwaj ran towards the walls, his hand reached for another arrow from his back and he took a running shot at one of the pigeons. The second arrow missed its target.

By now, the buffalo was just ten feet from the prince. Someone screamed, 'Give up, prince.'

Another spectator shouted, 'Ask them to open the escape grill. Now!'

But the prince didn't get distracted. Instead, he took a third shot, a second before the buffalo struck, and, after releasing the arrow, he leaped wildly to his right.

Strategically, he was right because just before the strike, a buffalo always lowers its head further and can't see what's in front. But the prince was a fraction of a second late, and one of the buffalo's horns pierced his left calf muscle. The beast dragged the prince by his leg for a few metres before shuddering to a stop. Then, it shook and jerked its horns, and the young prince went flying in the air and fell against a wall.

It was deathly quiet now. One could only hear the breathing of the bull and the cries of pain from the young prince. The pigeons had escaped into the sky as the third arrow had failed to find its target too.

The buffalo charged again. The prince tried to get up on his feet but lost his balance and fell down. The second time, he succeeded in standing up and tried to move towards the wall, limping badly. He was opening his mouth, perhaps to signal that he was giving up, but once again, he was a fraction of a second late as the buffalo pounced on him from behind. The beast's slanted horns entered the prince's back and came out from his chest. The animal then lifted its head, and with the young prince stuck on top of it, it flung him to one side as a haunting shriek echoed throughout the stadium. The prince didn't move after his body fell to the ground and came to rest. The buffalo didn't charge again. Everyone knew the prince was dead.

Lachit turned to look at Padmini. She sat expressionless, with her face pointed towards the middle of the arena. The next name was announced.

'Lachit Borphukan,' echoed in all directions.

Drummers started beating again, filling the air with anticipation once more.

For some reason, Lachit wanted Padmini to look in his direction and speak to him with her eyes and her smile. He wanted her to wish him luck. He needed it. But when she didn't look in his direction, he turned his attention to his parents. His father and mother were both looking at him. While his father's face was stiff and devoid of any visible emotion, his mother had tears in her eyes, though she appeared to be fighting them. Both of them raised their hands to bless him once again.

Lachit got to his feet and heard Chakradhwaj say, 'Best wishes, brother.'

He looked down at his best friend, smiled and replied, 'Thank you.'

As Lachit stepped into the arena, there was a loud roar from the spectators. Everyone knew he was the only son of the brave Borphukan, and today, they would witness first-hand if he was worthy of being called a Borphukan or not.

Lachit walked to the centre of the arena and pulled out an arrow. He mounted the arrow on the nocking point of the string and took a deep breath. This was the moment. He could feel the pressure. Guruji had said his strength was in water, but here he was on land. He closed his eyes and his entire life flashed by him in a few seconds. He thought of the prayers he had rendered in the name of the Kamakhya deity.

He opened his eyes and looked around. Thousands of pairs of eyes were trained on him. The movement of his head stopped when his eyes met Swargadeo's. The king's expression was inscrutable.

The next moment, the king broke eye contact and raised his hand for the guards to free the wild buffalo. Lachit heard the clang of the metal's lifting, but his eyes were now locked with Padmini's. She smiled just a little and nodded.

The buffalo walked out into the arena and spotted Lachit. Just then, the pigeons were released. Lachit pulled the string and took his first shot as the buffalo began charging towards him.

The arena reverberated with the sounds of the buffalo's hoofs hitting the ground and lifting clumps of grass, mud and dust. Lachit felt the sweat on his chest turn cold before it started to trickle down. He swallowed his panic and thought about his father. Moments later, courage rose in his gut and expanded in his chest. After it reached his mind, his features hardened and his posture altered to adjust to the bulge in his muscles. He was ready.

His eyes were on the approaching beast. That's when Lachit decided to do the unthinkable. Instead of targeting more pigeons, he charged at the buffalo.

Spectators jumped to their feet. Their eyes were wide, mouths hung open. *What was he doing*, everyone seemed to be wondering.

Lachit's arrow had pierced the pigeon and it fell down. But no one noticed the bird.

When Lachit was a few feet from a headlong collision with the buffalo, using the lower limb of the bow against the ground and the advantage of his forward momentum together with his powerful leg muscles, he leaped in the air.

Lachit's body missed the buffalo by a few inches and he landed behind it. The buffalo ran for a few metres more and then stopped. Meanwhile, Lachit took two quick shots and brought two more pigeons down.

The buffalo turned around. It was looking at its target. Lachit met the beast's gaze.

The pigeons were now quite high in the sky. Lachit flicked his head up, took quick aim and shot another arrow. As soon as he released the arrow, the buffalo began to charge at him again.

This time, Lachit didn't run towards the animal. He didn't try to escape out of the gate either. So far, he had successfully killed three pigeons. The fourth arrow was still in the air, but more than the dead pigeon count, the crowd was keener to know his next move.

Lachit glanced at Padmini. She smiled measuredly. From the steps, Chakradhwaj noticed this fleeting exchange. His expression was once again unreadable.

Lachit widened his legs, pulled out another arrow and, instead of aiming at the pigeons in the sky, he aimed at the charging beast. When the animal was around twenty feet from him, he released the arrow. A fraction of a second later, the arrow hit the buffalo in the right eye and the buffalo's head turned from the pain and the impact. Lachit stood his ground as the animal careened and, missing Lachit by a whisker, crashed into the wall with a loud thud. Just then, a pigeon with an arrow pierced through its body fell from the sky and landed on top of the beast.

The crowd roared and Padmini jumped to her feet and started to clap. It was Lachit's turn to smile now. His score was four pigeons. Borphukan and Yashodhara were on their feet too, clapping enthusiastically.

Lachit returned to his seat, and Chakradhwaj hugged him and slapped his back in brotherly affection.

'That was fabulous, Lachit.'

'Thank you, Chakradhwaj.'

The next competitor's name was announced, but he refused to participate and was disqualified. Over the next hour, other competitors tried their best to fight, but only a prince called Chung Mung could claim three pigeons, whereas others bagged two each. After Lachit's round, a new buffalo was used, which seemed to be slower than the one he had wounded.

Finally, it was Chakradhwaj's turn. Lachit wished him luck but he knew his best friend was the only one who could ruin his chances of being garlanded by Princess Padmini.

As Chakradhwaj took position in the centre of the arena, there was a loud roar from the spectators. Just as the cluster of pigeons was escaping, he took his first shot, and his arrow pierced two pigeons in one go. When the buffalo charged, he took aim and brought the third pigeon down. Chakradhwaj's performance so far had been nothing short of spectacular.

In the final second before the buffalo's horns could strike the young prince, Chakradhwaj leaped to his right and safely landed on his feet. The buffalo crashed into the wall.

Before the buffalo could get up, Chakradhwaj had his arrow pointed towards the sky. He was on the verge of claiming his fourth bird. While Lachit's performance was visually spectacular, Chakradhwaj's seemed as if he was in greater control.

Just before releasing the arrow, Chakradhwaj looked at Lachit and then at Padmini. Both were gazing at one another. As the buffalo charged at him, he took his shot and jumped to his left as the buffalo missed him once again. People's eyes went up the next second, and everyone realized that Chakradhwaj had missed the fourth bird. That's when the prince shouted for the escape grills to be opened and he bowed out.

It was clear: Chakradhwaj had deliberately missed the bird. Seeing the chemistry between his best friend and Padmini, he didn't want to stand in the way. But neither Lachit nor Padmini noticed his sacrifice.

In the next minute, Lachit Borphukan was announced as the winner.

The crowd roared. Lachit was smiling widely as he walked towards the king's section to be garlanded. He still had mud and bloodstains on his body. He looked like a wounded soldier who had just won a battle.

He stopped in front of Swargadeo and bent his knee to show his respect ceremoniously.

The king smiled and said, 'Young man, you have done a great job. I see a lot of promise in you. I had no idea a non-royal could defeat all the royals of our kingdom. Congratulations.'

'I mean no disrespect to any royal, Swargadeo. I was only following the teachings of my guru. And four is my lucky number.'

'Congratulations.' It was Padmini this time.

He turned towards her. Their eyes met and sparks began to fly again.

He took a step closer towards her, and as the crowd cheered, she garlanded him. Back in the crowd, Chakradhwaj sat expressionless. He had allowed Lachit to win but had he really wanted to do that? No one knew what was going on in his mind. Perhaps, he was himself not sure. All he knew was that he had allowed his friend to win because friendship for him was above everything else.

After hesitating for a few seconds, Chakradhwaj was able to overcome the emotions that were tormenting him inside. He finally smiled and began to clap louder than those around him.

———•———

The princess of the Ahom kingdom, Padmini, was the only daughter of Swargadeo Jayadhwaj Singha. Her mother, Queen Promila Debi, had passed away when Padmini was just five years old. Everyone in the palace and the kingdom knew that the king loved Padmini more than his life. But that possessiveness had deprived Padmini of the carefree life of a young girl. She was kept guarded, not allowed to attend court or mingle with anyone except her attendants, and going outside the palace was strictly prohibited for her.

The evening after the competition, Padmini was standing on the terrace of the women's wing of the palace, looking lost and gloomy. She was surrounded by a dozen or so female and eunuch attendants who were singing songs in praise of nature and the progenitor of the Ahom royals, the first king Sukaphaa, but Padmini was as lonely as ever.

The sun was about to set, and her round face glowed in the fading light. The radiance of her face and the elegance in her movements were unmistakable, but her big eyes were sad. The attendants continued regardless.

From where she sat, she could get a breath-taking view of the scenery all around. There was the river Brahmaputra on one side and the Rang Ghar on the other. Then there was the jungle right next to the palace, where the king's security oversaw the lions and tigers that roamed free and served to scare the spies and enemies who dared to approach the palace from that direction.

Something caught her eye among the trees of the jungle. It was a quick flash of light. The next second, there was another flash. Intrigued, she got up and moved towards the terrace parapet. She peered into the darkness. Nothing appeared for the next few seconds.

Although Padmini was sixteen, she had never stepped out of the palace or beyond the Rang Ghar. Ever since she was a child, she had wanted to explore the world outside the boundaries of the palace—the markets, the river, the jungle, the fields, the waterfalls, people's homes. However, as the princess, her father had explained, it was dangerous for her to step out. As she grew older, this frustrated her no end. She was desperate, but even her attendants and the eunuchs who took care of her had been tutored to dissuade her from talking about going out in the open.

Right now, Padmini wondered about the flashes of light she had seen. She turned around and noticed that all her attendants were busy singing and enjoying the music. From the corner of her eyes, another flash caught her attention.

She stared into the darkness and there were three flashes more in quick succession. And then there was darkness. Was it being done by someone on purpose? But she couldn't see anyone.

After a pause of a few seconds, there were four flashes again. She realized the count was four. And then again, after a few seconds, there were four more. There was someone out there sending a message to her because she knew, due to the lights on the terrace, her silhouette would be visible from afar.

Who could it be? And why only four flashes? Her mind drifted to earlier in the day, when she had garlanded Lachit Borphukan, the young man who had won the tournament. There was something in the way he had looked at her. For some reason, she thought she'd known him for a long time, and when her fingers had brushed his chest as she was garlanding him, she had felt something in her stomach.

That's when it struck her. The winner had capped four birds and had said that four was his lucky number. She saw four quick flashes of light again. Was it him? Was it Lachit trying to send her a message?

She noticed a movement among the trees now. There was a shadow there; no, in fact, there were two shadows. Slowly, the shadows moved outside and began to approach the palace. She was certain one of them was Lachit. But what if they were sighted by her attendants on the terrace?

Padmini moved from the parapet and called out to one of the attendants, 'I have a headache. I want all of you to leave me alone for some time.'

The attendant bowed and all the others followed her out. Padmini now ran towards the parapet and looked down. Indeed, it was Lachit, and he was looking up at her. She smiled and he smiled back. The person with him was the prince who had been the last participant in the competition and who could have defeated Lachit but he had lost in the final moment.

Lachit signalled that they wanted to come up. Thinking quickly, Padmini gestured to them to wait and walked to one side of the terrace, where clothes, put out to dry during the day, fluttered in the wind. She selected a few garments, returned to the same spot and, giggling with excitement, threw them down.

———•———

Chakradhwaj and Lachit picked up the clothes and walked to a corner. Chakradhwaj was the first to speak, 'Lachit, these are women's clothes.'

Lachit replied, 'Yes, but can you think of a better way?'

'You mean ... I mean ... you want me to wear these?'

'I want *us* to wear these'

'You have a reason, brother. You want to meet Padmini. But why me?'

'Because you are helping your brother.'

'Only if you promise to wear such clothes when I take you to meet my girlfriend.'

Lachit laughed and said, 'Yes, I promise.'

Five minutes later, wearing their new clothes, Lachit and Chakradhwaj reached the main entrance of the women's section of the palace on the other side. Two guards stood there, smoking and chatting casually.

'Now what?'

'Remember to swing your hips when you walk.'

Chakradhwaj elbowed him. Lachit winked mischievously.

Covering their heads with the chador, they walked past the guards.

One of the guards called out, 'Hey, stop! What are your names?'

Lachit and Chakradhwaj stopped, their backs facing the guard. All he could see were two women draped in mekhela and chador.

The guard asked again, 'I said, what are your names?'

If either of them replied, their voice would give them away.

That's when they heard a female's voice from the inside saying, 'I've called them. Let them through.' A woman with her face covered appeared at the gate.

Lachit and Chakradhwaj followed her inside. They had no idea who she was. What if she was not Padmini? They knew, as a princess, Padmini would not walk to the gate all by herself.

The woman stopped and opened a side door. They followed her in.

The room was dimly lit, but there was enough light to notice where they were. The woman lifted her veil. It was Padmini. But what was she doing in a maid's clothes? That's when it dawned on them. She had anticipated trouble at the gate and prepared for it. It was a smart move.

But now all of them were in servants' clothes. Which meant they could not go to the main chambers.

'Padmini!' Lachit embraced her.

She hugged him back instantly. It was as if they had known each other for a long time.

Chakradhwaj looked nervously here and there until Padmini turned and said, 'Hello, Prince Chakradhwaj.'

'Hello, Princess Padmini,' he greeted her back. 'I must leave you two alone and guard the door.'

With that, he walked closer to the door and stood next to it, looking out from the gap as the door was ajar.

'It is such a pleasure to meet you, Padmini.'

'Same here, Lachit.'

He moved closer to her. 'So, your life here must be very exciting with so many servants.'

'To tell you the truth, it is not.'

'Why not?'

'Do you know, I have never stepped out of my palace, and the Rang Ghar. Not even once. For me, this place is like a prison.'

'A prison?'

'Yes, I want to be a free bird. I want to see places, meet people, I want to live a normal life with friends, laugh with them, cry with them, celebrate life's moments.'

Lachit had not expected this. He didn't know what to say.

Padmini continued, 'Lachit, would you help me see the world?'

Once again, he didn't know what to say. He studied her face in the semi-darkness and said, 'We could take you out of here but your attendants would get to know and they would inform your father.'

'I will ask them not to tell anyone that I'm missing.'

'You think they will follow your instructions? What if they are caught? The king will spare your life, but he will certainly behead them.'

'You are being very pessimistic.'

By now, Lachit's and Padmini's faces were barely inches away from one another. He looked at her lips and felt her breath on his face. A hunger Lachit had never experienced before engulfed him. Without realizing it, he began to move closer to her.

That's when he felt a jab of pain in his back. He blinked, and the moment shattered, waking him up to the world around him. Lachit turned and realized Chakradhwaj had elbowed him. That's when he sensed Padmini move away from both of them.

Lachit said, 'I thought you were guarding the door?'

'And I thought you had decided to come here only to meet her.'

They heard Padmini speak from the door, 'I want to show something to both of you.'

Without waiting for their reply, she opened the door and cocked her head, indicating they follow her. Dodging the passing attendants, they gained access to the princess's room.

Padmini quickly locked the door and headed for the window. Lachit and Chakradhwaj stood next to her. Tears were now streaming down Padmini's cheeks.

Lachit was alarmed, 'What's wrong, Padmini?'

'Look out of this window. This is all I have seen in my entire life. This and whatever the terrace and the Rang Ghar can offer. Can you help me experience the world on the other side of that horizon, Lachit?'

Lachit extended his arms and took her hand. She turned towards him, and they stood together, face to face. He wiped her tears and said, 'But this is almost impossible, Padmini.'

She replied, 'Where there is a will, there is a way.'

He nodded, thought for a few seconds, pushed the fear that rose in his gut back in and said, 'Okay, I will show you the world beyond the horizon.'

Chakradhwaj inhaled deeply and said, 'Lachit, if you are thinking of taking the princess from here without her father's permission that will be a big crime.'

'I'm not committing any crime, Chakradhwaj, I'm only showing the world to the princess. I'll personally come here and hand her back to her father.'

'I don't think we will succeed in smuggling her out of the gate in the first place. The guards will catch us. Getting inside is always easy, Lachit, but going out is difficult, as you know.'

'Who's talking about using the gates?' Lachit winked.

'Okay, even if we somehow take her out of the palace, whenever you come back with her, the king will behead you.'

'We will think about that later, Prince Chakradhwaj.'

Lachit looked down from the window and smiled.

Ten minutes later, just as the attendants started to knock at the door of the princess's chamber, the three of them lowered themselves from the window, climbing down the rope that they had made with curtains, bedsheets and other materials.

When they reached the ground, they heard a loud noise. The attendants and guards had managed to break open the door. Lachit, Padmini and Chakradhwaj looked up one last time at their wide eyes and shocked faces at the window before running towards the jungle.

CHAPTER 4

⁓⁓⁓

They had sprinted for around four hundred metres when Padmini came to a halt. Lachit and Chakradhwaj stopped too. The first line of trees was still fifty meters away, but Padmini was out of breath.

Gulping for air, with her body bent forward, Padmini said, 'I can't run any more!'

In the distance, they could hear the sounds of palace guards shouting. The entire palace was lit up now.

For a few seconds, Lachit didn't say anything. He turned to look at Chakradhwaj, who was breathing deeply too.

Padmini straightened her back, her breath somewhat stable now, and said, 'We can't go to the jungle, Lachit. There are tigers and lions there. It's like committing suicide.'

Lachit anxiously looked in the direction of the approaching sounds and the blurry lamps of the search party. He said, 'Don't worry about the predators, Padmini. We have spears and swords stashed in the jungle.'

Chakradhwaj added, 'Also, we are trained how to tackle lions and tigers, princess.'

That's when they heard the barking of the dogs. The sounds from the dogs had detached from the other sounds and had started to move faster towards them.

Alarmed, Lachit turned and said, 'Come on, we must hurry up.'

He extended his hand, and when Padmini's palm clasped over his, he pulled her.

They started running again, the pack of barking dogs getting closer and closer with every passing second. Lachit was aware that they wouldn't be able to outrun the dogs. He also feared that the barking would alarm predators in the jungle. While running, he glanced at Chakradhwaj, and their eyes met briefly. They both knew that they would have to tackle their troubles one by one.

The best way to throw the dogs off their trail was by getting rid of their bodily scents. This meant they needed to reach the river before the dogs reached them. They could get in the river at one point and out at a different point downstream, their scent trails completely erased.

In the next fifteen minutes, after they had crossed a portion of the jungle, the dark water of the Brahmaputra lay ahead of them, shimmering in patches in the moonlight. By now, the dogs were just fifty feet behind them and closing in fast.

For a moment, Lachit thought they wouldn't be able to make it.

Through clenched teeth, he said, 'When I say jump, everyone jumps!'

The dogs were now just ten feet behind them and the water was still twenty feet away.

That's when Lachit shouted, his cry for help desperate, 'Bada bhai! Help!'

A dozen or so crocodiles surfaced and opened their mouths simultaneously a few feet from the shore. Padmini's eyes widened and her feet skidded to a halt. That's when Lachit picked her up and leaped over the crocodiles as their mouths opened. Chakradhwaj jumped over the crocodiles too.

The dogs stopped in their tracks. However, two of them couldn't break their momentum and leaped above the line of crocodiles. The crocodiles caught them mid-air in their mouths, their jaws slicing through them, killing them instantly.

The other dogs stayed back. The tone of their barking had changed and, slowly, they began to retreat in the direction from where they had come from, their tails between their legs.

By now, Lachit and Padmini had swum to the other side, where they lay, exhausted, on the muddy bank. Chakradhwaj was on his back too. All three of them were staring at the sky and catching their breaths. For the time being, they knew, it was safe behind the wall of crocodiles guarding the opposite bank.

After a few minutes, Lachit raised his head and saw the palace guards and the search party approach the river with lamps in their hands. Their steps were tentative as they must have encountered the retreating dogs.

He smiled at Padmini and said, 'We are safe now.'

She smiled, though half-heartedly. Then, she turned her head towards the crocodiles and raised her eyes, simultaneously bringing her finger to her lips, indicating to Lachit to be silent or the crocodiles might hear them and attack them.

'Don't worry, they are Lachit's friends,' said Chakradhwaj.

She looked at both her saviours and opened her mouth to say something but stopped.

His voice level, Lachit said, 'Prince Chakradhwaj is right. You don't have to worry about the crocodiles.'

The search party from the palace, comprising of guards, soldiers and attendants, had stopped at a safe distance from the line of crocodiles. They were now getting ready with their bows and spears. This was not a good sign.

'It's time to go,' Lachit said.

The three of them started to walk away as the crocodiles closed their mouths and dived back to the safety of the river, the barrage of arrows falling harmlessly on the surface of the water.

Five minutes later, walking through a quiet night now, Lachit, Padmini and Chakradhwaj reached a large tree.

Chakradhwaj approached a thicket of bamboos and pulled out a cloth bag. Inside were spears, bows and arrows and a few hengdang swords.

He handed over a hengdang to Padmini. She extended her hand, smiled and took it. But as soon as he moved his hand away, her hand, along with the sword, dropped down.

'Hey, careful with that, princess.'

Lachit took it out of her hands and stared angrily at his best friend, his eyes admonishing him silently. Chakradhwaj caught his ears between his fingers to complete the non-verbal communication, a hesitant smile on his lips.

So far, Chakradhwaj's behaviour had been odd. Though he had been pulled into the impromptu kidnapping of the princess of the Ahom kingdom as a result of his loyalty to his best friend, the way he looked at Padmini revealed he was attracted to her.

However, Lachit and Padmini continued to overlook this minor aberration in his behaviour. Even for Chakradhwaj himself, these were initial missteps that he was confident of overcoming soon. Friendship was still more important to him than love.

Lachit whistled, and two horses emerged from behind the trees. In the moonlight, the horses looked majestic as they trotted and halted next to their masters.

Lachit mounted the black horse and Chakradhwaj the white one. Lachit bent down and effortlessly lifted Padmini to her seat in front of him, her legs on either side of the saddle just like him.

The three of them faded into the night on their horses.

———•———

Back in the palace, Swargadeo Jayadhwaj Singha was shouting at the palace's security guards. Several guards and soldiers stood before him, their heads bowed. Some had dirt on their bodies as they had just returned from the river after their unsuccessful attempt to rescue the Ahom princess.

'All of you are good for nothing. Two strangers breached the security of our palace, entered the princess's quarters and kidnapped her. Then, they ran on foot and none of you could catch them. What should I do with you? Tell me?'

Everyone had been summoned to this midnight emergency meeting in the king's court. Although the king was shouting, there was a tinge of resignation in his voice.

He continued, his voice choking with emotion, 'I can't live without my daughter. You heard that … I can't live without Padmini. I want you to bring her back safely. Or, or … I will …'

Himabhas got up, looked at the others present and said, 'Swargadeo, I give you my word; we will do everything we can to get the princess back.'

The king kept on looking at the ground and didn't respond. Himabhas exchanged looks with Borphukan.

Now, Borphukan got to his feet and said, 'Using Himabhas's network of spies, and my soldiers, we will comb every tree, every pond, every river, every town and village and catch the two kidnappers.'

The two Gohains looked at one another. Then, Buragohain said, 'My king, the way the crocodiles saved them, we are of the opinion that these kidnappers are well-versed in black magic.'

Swargadeo Jayadhwaj Singha stood up and started to shout again, 'Don't tell me what you can do, you fools, do it …'

Even though the king was angry and had every reason to be so, his calling them fools was beyond protocol. The temper of the court leaders started to rise, but they remained patient as this was an extraordinary situation.

That's when the king broke down completely and started to cry like a child. He sat on the edge of his throne and slipped down to the carpeted floor.

Everyone, except the soldiers, exchanged looks. They felt a mix of pity, anger and frustration over the situation. Himabhas walked towards the king and said, 'Swargadeo, I beg you, please pull yourself together.'

He helped him get up. Once on his feet, the king jerked his arm free and, instead of going back to his throne, left the court. But he stopped at the royal exit behind the throne, paused for a few seconds, turned and spoke in a low voice, 'Don't call me unless you have brought my daughter back safely.'

After this, Swargadeo Jayadhwaj Singha, the king of the Ahom kingdom, locked himself in his royal chambers.

At that time, no one had any idea that the king would not emerge for two weeks.

———•———

Padmini had never seen or experienced so much nature around her in her life. As promised, Lachit showed her everything. At night, they sat near the shrubs of raat ki rani, the night-blooming jasmine, inhaling the sweet smell of flowers, watching the surroundings pigmented by dancing fireflies, as they cooked and ate freshly-caught fish from the Brahmaputra. During the day, Lachit taught her archery and the basic use of the hengdang as they hunted rabbits and partridges. In turn, Padmini taught him how to dance, play the flute using a bamboo stem and dress and eat like an Ahom royal, ignoring his protests that he was not a royal.

Chakradhwaj had moved on, saying he wanted to return to Naigaon, his father's territory, which was a part of the Ahom kingdom under Swargadeo Jayadhwaj Singha. It was difficult for Lachit to let him go because they had spent six years together. Chakradhwaj felt the same way, and their final embrace felt out of place.

Over time, Padmini and Lachit grew closer. One afternoon, while she waited for Lachit, who was cutting firewood from a tree, she was transported back to the days when she was a young girl. Although her father was always around, after the passing of Padmini's mother, the role of nurturing her was taken up by an elderly woman called Tapani.

Tapani was wise and caring. She spent her whole day with Padmini, not only taking care of her like a mother but also teaching her art, business, state affairs and history. At night, she would narrate beautiful stories of faraway lands, where young princes and princesses lived a life of love, facing the challenges of life together and solving them.

One day, Padmini had asked, 'Tapani, are these stories really true? Because, here in Jorhat, everyone says a girl should not have a dream. Her job is to wait for the right man to enter her life and reveal his dream, which then becomes her dream too.'

'My sweet little child, yes, that is how it is here in Jorhat. But it will all change one day.'

'How? Who will change it?'

'I don't know who will change it, Padmini. Perhaps, you will.' Tapani smiled and pinched Padmini's cheek.

Perhaps this was what Tapani had secretly wanted for herself. She might have fought for her dreams but given up in the end. Maybe, she'd wanted her fight to continue through the princess.

Padmini replied, 'I will change this, Tapani. I promise that I'll not give up my dreams.'

Tapani passed away a year after this conversation. A few hours before her death, Padmini visited her.

Tipani looked older and weaker than Padmini had ever seen her before. She said, 'My princess, Padmini, I will leave this world very soon. Promise me that you will fight, and if you don't succeed, you will obey your father. He's the Swargadeo of us Ahoms and he will help you find your destiny.'

With tears in her eyes, Padmini sat beside her, held her hand and said, 'Mother, I love you.'

Seeing Padmini affected by her condition, Tapani tried to smile and said, 'My sweet daughter, I have led a blessed life being your mother. I'm going away happy. So, don't worry about me, please.'

Padmini bent down and kissed Tapani's cheek, something she had never done. Even though Tapani had taken care of her like her mother, she was still a servant. That day, Padmini wanted her to leave the world thinking Padmini didn't consider her to be only a servant.

'I'm sorry to see you in pain like this.'

Tapani smiled and said, her voice faint, 'Don't worry about me, Padmini. Listen to me ... Your prince will come soon and he will show you the world.'

Then she closed her eyes. She never opened them again.

The next morning, when she was being cremated, Padmini had noticed Tapani's face was peaceful.

Tapani had taught Padmini the most important lesson— to make life meaningful, one only needs two things: love and courage.

Now, Lachit was back. He looked at her, snapped his fingers in front of her face and asked, 'Hey, love, where are you lost?'

Padmini broke out of her reverie and replied, 'I was thinking.'

He was holding a bunch of freshly-cut logs under his arm. He dropped them and asked, 'And what were you thinking?'

'I was thinking about Tapani, the woman who raised me like a mother, even though she didn't give birth to me.'

He raised his eyebrows, 'Tell me about her.'

Padmini looked away, blushed and said, 'She had said that one day a prince will come and take me away from the palace and show me the world.'

'Hmm ... she was right, except that I'm not a prince.'

'You are the prince of my heart, Lachit, and you will always be.'

He stared at her. Her hair was a lustrous black, their slight waves so mysteriously dark that they seemed to absorb the light around them and emit it through her face, making it look smoother and whiter than the finest porcelain.

He wanted to kiss her. The thought that had begun as a bubble in his mind turned into a balloon, and he had no option but to let it burst. He told her, 'You are very beautiful, Padmini, and I want to kiss you.'

She glanced up at him, her expression somewhere between pleasantly surprised and subdued annoyance. She raised her index finger and shook it, saying, 'No chance. First, you have to teach me everything that you know.'

Making the face of a young boy who had been denied a treat by his parent, he said, 'But, Padmini, it took me six years to learn these things.'

She replied, 'I'm a fast learner.'

He gave up for the time being.

One morning, after a hearty meal by the banks of the Brahmaputra, Lachit leaned forward and gently kissed Padmini's mouth. She looked at him, her eyes searching his face, and on realizing what he had on his mind, she pushed him away. As Lachit lost his balance and fell on his back, she moved away from him.

He leaped up on his feet and ran after her. Laughing, Padmini ran too.

Running through the filtered sunlight under the trees, she finally whistled just the way Lachit had taught her and the horse appeared.

. She held the saddle firmly and, in one swift motion, mounted the horse, her hands reaching for the reins. Then, she turned and waited for Lachit to get closer.

Lachit stopped ten feet from her, his hand raised, and said, 'All I want is a kiss, sweetheart.'

'Why?'

'You know why, Padmini. Because I love you.'

'I love you too, Lachit. But if you want the kiss, you have to come and get it.'

He smiled, his teeth gleaming, 'But if you run away like this, how will I get it?'

'Where there is a will, there is a way.'

As Lachit ran towards her, she gave a sharp tug at the reins, and the horse's forelegs went up in the air before it neighed and galloped away. There was no way Lachit could catch up with the animal, so he stopped, his hands raised.

That's when another horse crossed him and started to go after the princess. Lachit's eyes widened. He had no idea who this person was. All he could see was a man dressed in black following Padmini.

Lachit began to run after the stranger's horse. He knew, as a human, he could never chase a horse, so he turned and took a shortcut. He knew the route his horse would take. He cut across the narrow track and ran as fast as he could, ducking under low trees, jumping across ditches and skidding over grassy stretches until he emerged on the track again. But he missed the man chasing Padmini by a whisker. As he once again cut across the track, he caught Padmini looking back at the intruder behind her. There was fear in her eyes.

For a fraction of a second, Lachit's and Padmini's eyes met, before a tree obstructed his view as he continued to run. The next second, one of his legs was caught in a creeper, and he fell face down into a rotting cake of rhino dung. He was back on his feet and running once again, spitting out and shaking his head to dislodge the dung pieces stuck to his hair.

After a few seconds, he slipped and fell into a puddle of rainwater. He rose again, shook his head and started to run again.

The next time he emerged on the track, he was ahead of Padmini. He jumped, his hands grabbing the hanging root of a tree directly above him. After raising himself to a suitable height, he hung there, waiting.

As soon as Padmini's horse appeared, he set his eyes on it and, when her horse was under him, Lachit jumped and landed on it, right behind Padmini.

She turned to look at him. Tears were streaming down her cheeks and flying everywhere. Some of them fell on Lachit's face. He licked it and said, 'Salty!'

She smiled. Lachit pulled the reins even harder and the horse's pace increased. Within seconds, the distance between them and the intruder began to get bigger.

A turning appeared in the track right ahead of them. Holding Padmini, Lachit leapt off the horse. They landed on soft grass. Their horse didn't stop.

Lachit helped Padmini to her feet and whispered to her to hide behind a tree. Then, he drew his sword from its sheath and began to wait for the enemy's horse.

Soon, he heard the hoofbeat of the approaching horse. Lachit stood in the middle of the track. Since he was just beyond the sharp bend, he knew the enemy wouldn't be able to spot him until the last moment.

Lachit bent his knees and got into position, his senses alert. The sound of the hoofs hitting the ground was getting louder. He closed his eyes and mumbled a short prayer to Kamakhya Devi.

His eyes were wide in anticipation, his face taut and neck muscles flexed. The hair on his body bristled.

Who was this man riding a strange-looking horse, wearing a strange uniform and for how long had he been trailing them?

One thing was clear. He wasn't from the Ahom kingdom.

The sounds of the hoofs were even louder now. The enemy would be on him any second.

The horse sighted Lachit a fraction of a second before the intruder did. The animal tried to halt, neighing loudly, but the distance was too small. As the animal skidded, Lachit swung his sword, catching the horse's nose. It gave a guttural cry of pain, stopped and lifted its hind legs. The intruder fell from the horse. All this had happened in less than three seconds.

The man challenged Lachit in a language Lachit didn't understand. By now, he had partly overcome the shock of the fall and had pulled out his sword.

Lachit looked at the sword. It was longer than his hengdang, slightly more curved and had a knuckle bow.

The weapon immediately gave away the identity of the intruder. He was a Mughal soldier from the west. But what was he doing so deep into Ahom territory?

The man challenged Lachit to a fight. Lachit took a few steps forward and sliced the air with his hengdang. The Mughal soldier jumped back.

From behind the tree, Padmini was watching the fight. She was no longer the scared young woman she had been until a few moments ago. Now, her face had hardened. Lachit had left his bow and arrow next to the tree. She picked it up, her eyes on the two men. The Mughal soldier's sword had managed to nick Lachit's cheek, leaving a gash. Lachit had hit the soldier twice on his chest, but the metal armour had protected the enemy.

Padmini mounted the arrow and stretched the string. Then, after taking aim, she breathed in just the way Lachit had taught her the past couple of weeks, and when she felt confident, she released the arrow. She missed her mark. But the shot alarmed the enemy and he turned to look in her direction.

This was what Lachit needed—a distraction. His next strike caught the Mughal soldier on his neck. The sword fell from the soldier's hand, and he dropped to his knees. Lachit waited, his sword-wielding hand still in the air for his next strike. But the soldier fell and didn't move.

Using his leg, Lachit turned him around. The soldier appeared dead.

He waited. From the corner of his eye, he saw Padmini come closer. He raised a hand to stop her and gestured to her to go back behind the tree.

Lachit scrutinized his surroundings. It wasn't possible that this man had penetrated so deep into Ahom territory alone. *Where were his companions*, he wondered.

The day was quiet. He looked again at the soldier: a pool of blood had formed under his neck. The man was either dead or he was just laying still, praying for an opportunity.

Lachit waited for a few minutes before approaching him again, his sword drawn. The soldier was not dead but all the blood had drained from his face. He looked grey.

As Lachit bent down next to his head, the soldier opened his eyes. More than fear, there was resignation in them. He opened his mouth to say something, but blood trickled out of his mouth. His throat moved up and down a few times. The man was trying to say something important to Lachit, but all he could make were gurgling sounds. Even if he did say something, Lachit knew he wouldn't have understood his language.

With a final jerk, the wounded soldier breathed his last. Lachit searched his clothes and found a few coins. The coins confirmed he was a Mughal soldier.

He gently rubbed his eyes and took a deep breath. Then, he dragged the dead soldier to one side. Here, he dug a pit as Padmini waited. Finally, both of them rolled the dead soldier into his grave and lobbed his sword on top of him before covering the pit with earth again.

Later, back on his horse with Padmini seated in front of him, Lachit rode westwards for a couple of hours until they reached a cliff. Here, they dismounted from the horse and, holding its reins, Lachit walked up to the edge of the cliff with Padmini alongside him.

As he looked at the river that flowed beyond the cliff, Lachit's eyes widened. Anchored in the river was a large Mughal flotilla of over a hundred boats and ships.

'What does this mean?' asked Padmini.

A worried Lachit replied, 'It means war, bloodshed and that all of us should be ready to lay down our lives to protect the heavenly kingdom of the Ahoms from these devils of the west.'

She gasped, 'What are we going to do about it, Lachit?'

He turned to look into her eyes and said, 'We must go and warn the Swargadeo, your father, and prepare for war.'

CHAPTER 5

Outside Jorhat, 1640

Borphukan's birthname was Momai Tamuli. His father was a paik, a simple man who wore his uniform for three months every year and worked in the Ahom army. He was a man of music and loved eating and dancing.

One evening, when Momai was around ten, his father asked him, 'Momai, what do you want to be when you grow up?'

The little child, who until then had never moved more than a kilometre away from their little bamboo hut that sat on a small hillock overlooking the Brahmaputra, didn't know what he wanted to become, and so he said, 'I want to become a paik like you, Father.'

His father smiled. He had been silently praying for an answer along those lines. He said, 'We are a family of soldiers and there's nothing more honourable than to lay your life for the protection of your motherland.'

His father then started to sing and dance around little Borphukan. For the little child, as his answer made his father so happy, becoming a soldier became his solitary ambition ever since.

Hearing the singing and laughter, his mother came out of the hut and watched them, a gentle smile on her face. She was a shy woman, deeply devoted to taking care of Momai and his father.

When his father spotted her, he pulled her towards him and started to dance with her. She was embarrassed initially but gave in at the end, moving her body with his song. Within minutes, more people joined the celebration from nearby huts, and a few of them had started to play musical instruments as well. All this just because little Momai had said that he wanted to become a soldier.

A few days later, Momai's father took the young boy to Jorhat for a fair. He had never been to the capital and he had been wide-eyed from the time they reached its massive gates.

'Father, this gate is soooo biiiig ...' he exclaimed.

At the fair, there were jugglery performers in colourful clothes, angry animals in locked metal cages, magicians with painted faces and a small market where food, clothes and gifts were being sold. There was music, there was laughter and there were animated screams of excitement from the children and adults who went around witnessing and participating in the various activities.

Momai had never seen so many people in his life before. Everyone had a wide grin on their face, and children, both younger and older than him, ran from one show to the other.

They had decided to watch the magic show first. Momai watched a magician make a pigeon disappear into thin air and pull out a ribbon from Momai's ears. *How is this possible*, he wondered, laughing. The magician remarked, 'You must have eaten it for breakfast.' Everyone, including Momai's father, laughed.

They moved to the next enclosure to watch the famous monkey show. A male and a female monkey danced and behaved as humans do. It was funny but also cute.

Later, they walked through the market and ate fried food, skewered meats and sweets. Momai's stomach got so full that he could hardly breathe. He remarked, 'I have never eaten so much.'

In response, his father ruffled his hair and they moved ahead.

Before returning home, his father wanted to buy his son a gift, so he stopped in front of a shop and suggested, 'Momai, would you like to wear a paik's uniform?'

He responded innocently, 'You mean … take it home?'

As his father sat outside and smoked, little Momai accompanied the shopkeeper inside and pointed at the uniform he liked.

'Would you like to try it?' The shopkeeper asked.

Unsure, he craned his neck to check with his father but couldn't spot him outside.

The shopkeeper reassured him, 'It's okay. You can try it if you want.'

Momai put on the uniform that he had selected. The shopkeeper held his hand and took him to the mirror. Momai faced the mirror and saw his reflection. Wearing the uniform, tiny boots, and a safa, he looked like a child soldier.

The shopkeeper also gave him a tiny hengdang and a shield. That's when his father stepped inside the shop. His jaw dropped as he looked at his son. He said, 'Son, please take this off immediately.' Then, he turned to the shopkeeper and said, 'What are you doing? I want to buy a paik's uniform for him, not a Borphukan's uniform.'

'What's a Borphukan, Father?' Momai asked his father.

'Err ... it's the General of all the paiks.'

Momai smiled and said, a childlike twinkle in his eyes, 'Father, I want to become the Borphukan.'

The father looked at his son, speechless. His son had said something that wasn't possible.

The shopkeeper waited for the father to say something, and when he didn't, he filled in, 'Son, you can become the Borphukan if you want to. Everything begins with wanting.'

His father paid for the uniform. On their way back home, his father was quiet. After they reached home, Momai's mother asked him, 'What happened? Why this gloomy face?'

The little boy replied on his father's behalf, 'Father is angry because I want to become the Borphukan.'

His father turned to look at him. He had tears in his eyes as he said, 'My dear son, my sweet little Momai, I am not angry with you. I'm sad because you have said something that's not possible. We are poor farmers and all we can hope for is to become paiks.'

'Father, I will become the Borphukan one day.'

His father raised his hand, placed it on the boy's head and said, 'I bless you, my son. May you become the Borphukan of the Ahom army one day.'

———•———

Jorhat, 1664

Borphukan gazed at the painting of his father that hung in the main hall of his palace and whispered, 'Father, your son, the son of a paik, could become a Borphukan because of your blessings. And now, your grandson, Lachit, is ready to become the next Borphukan. Please bless him too, Father.'

Yashodhara entered the hall and saw her husband standing with folded hands in front of his father's painting. She walked to him and stood next to him, joining him in prayer.

Borphukan sensed her arrival and turned around. Their eyes met. She smiled.

Borphukan said, 'Do you know, Yashodhara, what I miss the most in my life?'

She nodded. 'That your father could not see you as the Borphukan before he left the world.'

'Yes.' His voice was distant. Then, he turned with purpose and said, 'But because of my father's blessings, I will watch our son Lachit wear the Borphukan's uniform soon.'

She nodded.

They walked towards the seating area. Mattresses and cushions were arranged around a low table with a large plate of fruits on it. There were slices of litchi, mango, papaya and plum.

Borphukan took a deep breath and said, 'I've been the Borphukan of the Ahom army for twenty years now. Without you by my side, I would have been totally lost, Yashodhara.'

She replied, 'Hmm … you know, when I was a girl, my father, the Borphukan that everyone in the Ahom kingdom dreaded, wanted me to marry the next Borphukan. And that's all I had dreamed of, so when I was sixteen, when I saw the man who would be the next Borphukan at a fight in the Rang Ghar for the first time, I knew he would be my husband soon.'

Borphukan's mood changed as the sides of his mouth turned up, 'You are making me jealous, sweetheart.'

'Well, that was in the past, and now I have been all yours for life.'

He leaned forward, kissed her gently on her lips and said, 'I love you, Yashodhara. Thank you for agreeing to marry me.'

She raised her eyebrows, 'You didn't give me an option, did you? Even as a Hazarika, you were noticed for your courage by my father, and he pitched you in a do-or-die battle against the man everyone thought I would marry.'

'Did that upset you?'

'I will tell you what I have always told you because that is the truth. Yes, it initially pained me no end. I thought, what was my father up to?'

'And yet you arrived at the Rang Ghar.'

'Yes, I did. Because everyone said he would win. You stood no chance. You were the underdog ... but the first time I saw you, I knew what was going to happen. I knew why my father wanted this fight. I immediately knew that my father had begun to doubt the capability of that man. But he wanted to prove what he had in mind in front of twenty thousand pairs of eyes.'

'You know, I was shocked when I was told I had to fight with the man who was about to be elevated to the post of Borphukan. I thought my fate was to die at the Rang Ghar so that no one would challenge his candidature. I was the scapegoat, a deer that your father needed to sacrifice to prove a point.'

'That's what you felt?'

'The day before our duel, I remember very vividly, your father had come to meet me.'

She was startled. 'You have never told me this part, honey.'

'Well, he promised me that I shouldn't share the news of his visit with anyone, particularly with you.'

'This is interesting … so, tell me what happened.'

'I was expecting you to ask why I am telling you this now if I had given your father my word that I wouldn't.'

'Okay, tell me, why are you telling me now after so many years?'

'That's because I saw him in a dream the other day. He said he was proud of the way I have defended the Ahom kingdom, and of how the two of us have raised Lachit and prepared him to become the next Borphukan.'

She looked into the distance and said, her voice low, 'I'm waiting for him to appear in my dream too … Perhaps, I need to perform ancestor worship with greater devotion.'

'Perhaps.'

'So, yes, what did he say when he met you the day before the duel?'

Borphukan's face softened as he reminisced. 'Your father said I deserved to become the Borphukan more than my competitor. And then he said …'

Yashodhara bent closer.

'… he said, if I won, he would get you married to me. I was shocked. No words came out of my mouth. He further said, "My daughter's name is Yashodhara. She will be there to watch the duel tomorrow, and you can easily identify her." I waited for him to say more and after a pause he did: "The most beautiful girl in the stadium will be Yashodhara," adding, "you can't miss her."'

Yashodhara had tears in her eyes. 'My father was so, so special. You should have told me this before.'

'And broken my promise?'

'Yes, don't you remember what the priest had said during our wedding ceremony … that there should be no secrets between husband and wife.'

'This secret was different.'

She hugged him and said, 'I know, I was just kidding. My father was the greatest father in the world, and now I'm married to the greatest husband in the world.'

'And our son will soon be the greatest Borphukan of the Ahom army.'

'Yes, by the blessings of Kamakhya Devi, he will be.'

After they were quiet for a couple of minutes, she said, 'What did you feel when you first saw me at the stadium?'

He teased her, 'I have told you so many times.'

'But I want to hear it again.'

'Hmm … so I was ready with the sword in my hand. It was just a few moments before my competitor arrived.

That's when my eyes fell on you. Your father was right. You were the most beautiful woman. You shone like a beacon.'

'You found the final bit of courage to fight because you saw me, didn't you?'

'Yes, I did. But when my competitor stepped into the arena, I forgot everything.'

She pushed him, feigning to be annoyed, as he continued, 'All I could think of was how to defeat the enemy.'

'I remember. That fight was very bloody, but you killed him in the end.'

'Yes, the crowd couldn't believe it. I couldn't believe it. There was silence for a few moments before someone from the crowd started to clap, and within seconds, the whole stadium was celebrating the win.'

'What if I told you I was the person who clapped first?'

He smiled, 'I would believe you.'

'By the way,' Yashodhara's expression changed as she said, 'Lachit said he's going to the mountains to spend time with his friends. But it's been three weeks. Did he tell you when he would be back?'

Borphukan shook his head. 'No, he didn't. But he's a grown man now. Let him have his share of fun. I'm sure he will be back soon.'

———•———

Lachit and Padmini rode non-stop on their horse until they reached Jorhat. Their personal safety and need for adventure had been overshadowed by the imminent threat the Ahom kingdom faced. After accounting for the time taken for them to reach the capital, Lachit thought Swargadeo would have six to eight hours to put the city's defence in place.

When they reached the gates of the capital, the guards recognized Padmini and let them through. Crossing three more inner rings of security, Lachit and Padmini finally reached Swargadeo Jayadhwaj Singha's court.

But there was no sign of the king. The court was being presided over by Himabhas and, except for Borphukan, Lachit's father, all the other members of the court were in attendance, including the two Gohains. Chakradhwaj and other princes were present as well.

As soon as Lachit and Padmini entered the court, Himabhas stopped speaking in mid-sentence. He got to his feet, and seeing him, everyone present turned and stood up too.

Lachit and Padmini started to walk towards Himabhas. Their hair was dishevelled and their faces flushed red due to nervousness, exhaustion and anxiety.

Lachit asked, 'Where is Swargadeo?'

'Arrest him!' Himabhas ordered the guards.

Lachit protested, 'Honourable Prime Minster, there is no time for this. Where is the king?'

Himabhas looked at the others and said, 'Swargadeo has no time for criminals like you.'

Padmini spoke now, 'Our kingdom is under attack.'

No one paid attention to her. Meanwhile, the guards had surrounded Lachit, and the tips of their naked hengdangs were barely millimetres from his throat.

Instead of getting scared and holding still, Lachit's eyes were searching for his father in the court.

Himabhas said, 'Guards, stop him right there. I'll call the Swargadeo. He will decide this kidnapper's punishment.'

That's when the door behind the throne swung open and Swargadeo Jayadhwaj Singha walked in. Everyone was shocked. All the hair on his head had turned completely grey.

'Swargadeo, your hair …' It was Himabhas.

Ignoring him, the king spotted his daughter and extended his arms. She ran towards him and melted into his embrace.

Lachit raised his voice, 'Swargadeo, our kingdom is about to be attacked. The enemy is just a hundred miles from the capital. You must call Borphukan and order him to prepare for war.'

'Shut up!' The king shouted, his voice booming across the court hall.

Padmini opened her mouth, 'Father, we have seen it ourselves.'

He turned towards her and opened his mouth to say something but changed his mind. He looked back at Lachit and said, 'Aren't you Borphukan's son, who won the competition?'

Lachit nodded.

'I never thought the son of the man who heads our military will stab us in the back and kidnap the princess.'

Padmini said, 'Father, we love each other.'

This time, he shouted at her too, 'Shut up! Are you out of your mind? How is this possible? This man is not a royal.'

This was not the discussion Lachit had expected. He tried again, 'Swargadeo, I urge you to prepare our army and the navy. The enemy will be here in a few hours.'

'You are the enemy … whatever your name is …' He turned towards the prime minister and ordered, 'Himabhas, I want this devil to be beheaded right now.'

Padmini gasped. Weeping, she said, 'Father, it is not what you think. I had asked him to take me. And nothing has happened between us.'

Her eyes fell on Chakradhwaj and she begged, 'Prince Chakradhwaj, please tell them the truth.'

Chakradhwaj cleared his throat and said, 'Swargadeo, the truth is, I'm equally at fault. Lachit and I had taken the princess for a few days because she wanted to go outside the palace and experience life, something you wouldn't allow her to do. And now she is back. Lachit is not at fault. He is, in fact, our best-trained warrior.'

Swargadeo considered this for a few moments before he looked at Lachit and said, 'I'm sparing your life for the first and the last time, okay? But I want you out of the capital. If my soldiers spot you in Jorhat, they will have orders to kill you. Now, get out of my sight.'

Lachit looked at Padmini and Chakradhwaj one final time and left.

The king dismissed the court after Lachit was gone. Guards accompanied Padmini to her royal chambers.

Dazed with the way things had played out and still processing the forced separation from Padmini, Lachit left the capital without meeting his parents. For him, as a duty-bound citizen, obeying the king's command was his top priority. He galloped out of Jorhat on his horse, taking the shortest route.

———·———

Six hours later, the Ahom kingdom came under a severe attack by the Mughals. The entire kingdom was caught unawares. Not taking Lachit and Padmini's warning seriously was going to cost them dearly.

As the Mughal sowars, the cavalry, breached the main gates of the capital, they were met with mixed resistance by the ill-prepared Ahom soldiers who hadn't had the time to reach the armoury to draw bombs, spears, swords, shields and bows and arrows. The hungry Mughal army started their indiscriminate killing and looting of the historic city.

By the time the brave Borphukan reached the gates and started to reorganize the resistance, it was already too late. The Mughal soldiers had infiltrated the capital and spread all around.

From his position, Borphukan saw the Mughal army breach the security cordons one after the other. The Ahom soldiers fought desperately but the sheer number of the Mughal soldiers was hard to contain. Borpukhan tried his best to motivate his soldiers but the speed with which the Mughal army rampaged and advanced towards the royal palace was something even he had not experienced in his life.

He changed his strategy and decided to defend the inner city that had the palace, the royal gardens, the horse and elephant stables and the armoury. As he mobilized the resources in the quickest possible time, Borphukan prepared the final layer of security.

Meanwhile, the Mughal army continued to push ahead, towards the palace.

Borphukan was shocked and thought, *how could all our spies fail? If only I had an advanced warning of just a few hours.* He had no idea that his own son Lachit and the king's daughter had warned the king six hours in advance but nobody had taken them seriously.

Inside the palace, Swargadeo was seated on his throne and his close advisors, including Yashodhara, were seated opposite him. All were quiet.

Ever since the king had learnt about the attack on the capital, he had been drinking luk-lao. Every few minutes, a soldier would run inside and report the falling of another line of defence as the Mughal army bulldozed forward on their way to the palace.

Himabhas said, 'Swargadeo, we should have listened to Princess Padmini and Lachit.'

He waved his hand, rejecting the suggestion.

His eyes half-closed from drunkenness, the king said, 'That bastard Shaiva sadhu, he has cursed us. I want you to find out where he is and behead him.'

Himabhas looked at the king, his face filled with frustration.

The king continued, 'Look! All my hair has turned grey because of him. How could he do this?'

Yashodhara said, 'Swargadeo, I wish you had taken the warning by Lachit and Padmini seriously. I have been told that they had come to warn you earlier during the day.'

He glared at her and said, 'But your son is a criminal. He kidnapped my daughter. I thought the warning was fake. Maybe he wanted to kidnap me too and declare himself as the king.'

She persisted, 'What about Padmini? Why didn't you take her warning seriously?'

He gave a smirk, 'Your son has poisoned the mind of my daughter. Be happy that I spared his life.'

Yashodhara swallowed her anger.

At that moment, another soldier entered, bowed before the king and said, 'Swargadeo, the Mughal army has stopped.'

The king raised his head in hope. Himabhas and the others eyed the soldier suspiciously.

'That's good news, isn't it?' The king exulted.

The soldier continued, 'We have not stopped them, my Swargadeo. They have chosen to stop, and now they are raping young Ahom women.'

The king got up and shouted, 'What? This is unacceptable. Bring me my hengdang!'

In his fervour, he slipped and fell down. His safa rolled to one side. He lifted his head.

Himabhas and the others had never seen a more pathetic sight. The enemy was raping young women and killing men just a few kilometres from the palace and the king was so drunk that he couldn't even lift a sword.

Himabhas helped the king onto the throne again and said, 'My Swargadeo, I think you should send a message for a truce. That way, we can save our dignity, at least partially.'

The king nodded.

Himabhas quickly wrote a note, made the king sign it and sent it through a soldier to the Mughal General. Now, all they could do was wait.

———•———

Right outside the palace, Borphukan was guarding the final security perimeter along with his soldiers. *This is it*, he thought. There was no way he could stop the hundreds of Mughal soldiers with a handful of his favourite Ahom paiks, but the Mughals would have to go over his dead body and the dead bodies of his soldiers to reach the palace. They would fight till the last drop of blood in their veins was shed.

He looked around at his soldiers. These were the best. He knew each one of them by name as he had trained them personally and led them into many battles.

The Mughals were in for a shock. They might have taken over the city due to the element of surprise, but here was where they would lose the most men. In the end, because of their numerical superiority, the Mughals would win, but the Ahoms wouldn't have given up their king without fighting. As the soldiers looked at Borphukan unfazed, he smiled at them in reassurance.

The soldiers of the Mughal army started to arrive. They stopped at a safe distance from Borphukan and his men to organize themselves and assess the situation.

Borphukan estimated their number to be around a thousand. Compared to that, the Ahoms defending the palace were only one hundred. He waited.

As the Ahoms watched, the Mughal formation parted at the centre and a huge horse trotted out. This was the largest horse Borphukan had seen in his life. The General of the enemy sat on it. Except for his eyes and mouth, all parts of his body were either covered in overlapping metal plates sewn to his clothes to form an armour or in protective leather covers. On his head, he wore a metal helmet. The body of the horse was also covered with overlapping metal plates.

The Mughal General surveyed the palace in front of him and smiled when he met Borphukan's eyes. He pulled out a white flag from the side of his saddle and waved it towards Borphukan. Then, he looked back at one of his soldiers and nodded. The soldier took the white flag from him, along with what looked like a piece of cloth, and started approaching Borphukan.

Borphukan was surprised at the development.

The soldier who was stationed on his right asked, 'The enemy is waving a white flag of peace … What does this mean, Borphukan?'

Without looking at him, Borphukan replied, 'This must be a trick.'

The soldier on his left spoke this time, 'Maybe they are tired and want to buy time by using these delaying tactics.' Then, he added, gritting his teeth, 'Or, maybe, they are scared of the ferociousness of our final line of defence.'

Borphukan didn't reply. His eyes were on the messenger who had by now covered half the distance between the Mughal soldiers and the Ahom line of defence.

Borphukan raised his right hand towards his soldiers and closed his fist. It was a visual signal ordering them to hold their weapons.

The Mughal soldier stopped where Borphukan was and gave him the piece of cloth. As Borphukan started to read it, his eyes widened. The cloth was signed by Swargadeo. It was his declaration that he was giving up.

Borphukan felt cheated and angry. He felt like shouting at the top of his voice. While he and his soldiers were ready to lay down their lives for the Ahom empire, the king had decided on a compromise only because he was scared of dying! *What a shame*, he thought.

Borphukan had no option but to order his men to let the Mughals through. After all, it was the king's order.

As the Mughals passed Borphukan, he had tears in his eyes. He had never felt more helpless in his life. As he avoided meeting the eyes of his soldiers, he felt that the surrender was worse than death.

CHAPTER 6

The Mughal General led his military formation to the palace, unopposed. Once he reached the palace gates, he stopped and got down from his horse. Then, with his selected bodyguards, he walked inside while all the others waited outside.

The General was a tall man who walked rigidly due to the heavy body armour. He had removed the helmet now and one could see his weather-beaten, full-bearded face. He was caked in dirt and grime, which meant he had been leading his troops from the front. His eyes were mean and narrow and his long hair was stuck on his head due to sweat. A jagged scar started from one side of his left eyebrow and disappeared under his beard.

Silence hung heavy in the air. The only sounds were of the General and his bodyguards walking.

The chill of the previous night was still trapped within the court's stone walls, though outside it was sunny and warm.

The General reached the king's throne and stopped around ten feet from it. His bodyguards stopped behind him. Then, using his index finger, he indicated to the king to get up. Swargadeo got up silently and stepped down.

The Mughal General sat on the throne and looked down at the Ahom leaders before him.

Swargadeo signalled to Himabhas with his eyes. Himabhas nodded and announced, 'The great Mughal General, we welcome you to Jorhat. First, as a mark of respect, we want to present our ceremonial gifts.'

A guard approached the General with an ornamental tray that had a xorai with a tamulpan placed in it and a neatly-folded silk gamosa kept next to it.

The General picked up the xorai and spat into it. Then he took the gamosa, dropped it on the ground and placed his soiled shoes on it.

He looked up and smiled. His teeth were surprisingly white, though it was clear that he had not had a proper bath for several days.

The guard took the tray away. Himabhas looked at Swargadeo. The Mughal General had dishonoured the sacred and ceremonious gifts of the Ahoms. The Swargadeo was staring at the floor.

The General opened his mouth to speak, 'You have done the wise thing by giving up. From this moment onwards, the Ahom kingdom is an ally of the mighty Mughal empire.'

Himabhas looked at the king, and when he didn't speak, he said, 'We will be happy to be an ally of the Mughal kingdom but we want to maintain our freedom.'

'You can continue as before. We want only two things. First, half of the kingdom's earnings should reach our capital in Agra every six months. And, second, we want the hand of Padmini. We have heard a lot about her beauty, and the Mughal emperor has sent this message through me that he would like her to join the emperor's harem.'

Jayadhwaj shouted, 'No, Padmini will not go anywhere. She is my daughter.'

The Mughal General laughed. 'Of course, she will. She is now a beautiful woman and she deserves the love and the seed of our emperor, so that she can bear his children.'

'No,' Jayadhwaj began to weep.

'I accept this proposal,' a woman's voice echoed through the hall.

Everyone turned their heads. It was Padmini.

'Oh, you are indeed stunning, princess,' said the General.

'But there is one condition. I want you to stop the looting and raping right away.'

He smiled and asked, 'What if we don't?'

She pulled a knife she was hiding behind her and placed it on her neck, 'Then I will kill myself right now.'

He laughed, 'I like the spark. I'm sure you will soon become the emperor's favourite.'

The deal was finalized in the next hour, and the king signed the treaty of accession. It was written in both Persian and Ahom's Brahmi script.

After that, the Mughal soldiers climbed the top of the palace and replaced the Ahom flag with the Mughal one. The Ahom flag was replaced at the capital's gates too.

With a heavy heart, the king embraced his daughter for the final time before she walked away from the palace with the Mughals. The Mughals stood behind her in an open chariot, so that the Ahoms could see their honour being taken away.

As Padmini stood in the chariot, she kept her face straight. There were no tears in her eyes and her expression was unreadable. When they reached the gate at the outskirts of the city, Padmini was shifted into a palanquin, and the Mughal army started to move towards the river in smaller groups.

———•———

Hiding in the jungle, Lachit had been restless for the past few hours. He knew that the Ahom army was ill-prepared and they would be routed soon. As an Ahom, it caused him endless pain, but there was nothing he could do.

Lachit had bribed an Ahom citizen from the capital to find out the outcome of the attack. That man had just informed Lachit that the Mughals were taking Padmini away. This was a big blow, and his helplessness multiplied. He decided to move as close to Jorhat's gate as possible.

Hiding from his position, an hour later, just outside the capital's gate, he watched the Mughals escort a palanquin.

It had to be Padmini in it. He counted ten Mughal soldiers, three on either side of the palanquin and two each at the front and the back.

He had also learnt that the Mughals had not departed from the capital in one large group but in a few smaller groups. Since the Ahoms had already given up, they were not expecting resistance on the way.

Staying out of sight, Lachit started to shadow the soldiers. Their route was known to him. He was aware that Padmini would be first taken to the riverhead, from where they would transfer her to a ship. That was where he would strike—on the edge of the water.

The party came to a stop at the banks of the river. A royal boat with four more soldiers was waiting for them. This was not good news for Lachit because now he would have to silence fourteen soldiers. He knew that a rescue attempt would be extremely risky as the next group of Mughal soldiers was expected to reach that spot in ten minutes. This meant Lachit needed to neutralize all the fourteen soldiers currently at the site within six minutes, help Padmini escape from the palanquin in one minute and then have at least a three minute head start before others arrived.

Lachit had four spears, two dozen arrows and two hengdang swords with him. He crouched behind a rock and waited for the right opportunity.

The Mughal soldiers were relaxed. As soon as they arrived, they started to smoke and chat.

From a distance, Lachit first used the spears and brought three soldiers down. Then, as they panicked and the soldiers on the boat abandoned their vessel and approached the palanquin, he used his arrows to kill four more. The group panicked, and three soldiers jumped into the boat and started to row away. Another one ran towards the jungle.

But the remaining three held their ground and, as Lachit charged towards them, they attacked back with their swords drawn.

For the next three minutes, Lachit and the three Mughal soldiers fought with their swords. It was a spectacular sight as sparks flew when metal struck metal. One of Lachit's swipes sliced through the leg of a soldier, and he fell down, crying in pain. Seeing this, another one ran away. But the last one stayed and was proving to be difficult to beat.

In the back of Lachit's mind, the clock was ticking. He fought valiantly. Finally, he succeeded in bringing the man standing between him and Padmini down. His mental clock indicated he had around two minutes remaining before the next group of soldiers arrived.

Whistling for his horse, he ran towards the palanquin and pulled the curtain aside. Padmini's eyes locked with Lachit's.

He was out of breath as he said, 'Come out, Padmini, let's go.'

Her eyes widened with relief. 'Oh, my love, did you come to rescue me? I will never forget this.'

'There is no time, Padmini. Let's get out of here.'

She closed her eyes to prevent tears from escaping and said, 'No, Lachit.'

'What? No? Step out. We need to leave now.'

She opened her eyes and her tears slid down, 'No, I can't come with you. I have to honour the Swargadeo's treaty. I have to honour my father's word. Turn around and see.'

Lachit turned, and in the distance, he could see the Mughal flag flying on the Ahom capital's gates.

'I belong to the Mughals, Lachit.'

Lachit's voice cracked as he said, 'But, I love you, Padmini. Without you, without you …'

'I'm not going away forever, Lachit. I will come back.'

He shook his head. 'How is that possible?'

Now, Lachit had tears in his eyes too. He stood there, his body limp, his cheeks stained with tears and his sense of urgency lost.

Padmini tried to smile. 'Where there is a will, there is a way.'

In the distance, they heard sounds. The next group was about to arrive.

Padmini placed her hands over Lachit's and said, 'Go. You *have* to save the Ahom kingdom, Lachit. You *have* to live.'

She pushed him away. Lachit turned and climbed onto his horse. The next second, he was riding away.

The Mughal General reached the scene. He looked around at the dead soldiers. Then he pulled the curtain of the palanquin to one side and was relieved to find the princess there.

'What happened?' He asked.

Padmini said, 'Someone was trying to rescue me. But I refused to go.'

He stared at her blankly, unsure what to say.

She smiled and added, 'I'm now a part of the Mughal empire, and we Ahoms never break a promise.'

He closed the curtain.

———•———

Swargadeo Jayadhwaj Singha was on his bed in his personal chamber at the palace. His eyes were closed. During the last twelve hours since Padmini was taken away, he had neither spoken nor eaten anything.

The chamber's door opened slightly and an old man entered. After taking a few steps, he stood there, as if uncertain what to do next.

'My Swargadeo,' he called out hesitantly.

There was no reply.

He walked towards the bed and stopped next to where the king's head was.

He whispered, 'My Swargadeo, I'm the vaid … I am here to make you feel better.'

The king stayed quiet.

The vaid nervously looked around the majestic room and his eyes came to rest upon the king again.

Tears flowed from the corner of the king's eyes. The vaid tried to imagine what the king was feeling. He was probably awake but too heartbroken to open his eyes. The mighty Ahom kingdom had been crushed and there was no one who could save them from the Mughal's enslavement.

He bent forward and felt the king's pulse. It was weak. He knew he had to react quickly, but before he could decide which herbs to prescribe, he needed to ask a few questions so that his diagnosis was accurate.

'My Swargadeo, how are you feeling now?'

There was no reply.

'Are you in pain? Can you tell me which part of the body is paining?' He paused for a few moments and asked again, 'Are you feeling tired?'

There was no reply to any of his questions.

After staying silent for a few moments, he rushed to the door and stepped outside. Here, besides the vaid's assistants and the palace priest, Prime Minister Himabhas was present too.

He approached Himabhas and spoke, his eyes cast down at the feet of the minister, 'Honourable Prime Minister, Swargadeo is not saying anything, and his pulse is weak.'

Himabhas said, his voice on edge, 'You are the Swargadeo's personal vaid. You know his body well. So, don't just stand there, do something quickly.'

The vaid bowed and stepped closer to his assistants. Himabhas saw them have a quiet conversation, after which they opened the door of the Swargadeo's chamber and disappeared inside.

After they were gone, Himabhas looked at the priest. The priest was around fifty, obese and his naked torso above the suria was sweating due to the pressure of the moment.

Himabhas said, 'I want you to start the yagna immediately.'

The priest bowed and left for the terrace of the palace, where all the royal ceremonies were conducted.

Inside the chamber, the vaid realized that the king's pulse had weakened further. A king who used to talk so much had stopped talking completely. It wasn't a good sign. He ordered his assistants to ground a few herbs. They took out a mortar and pestle along with the barks and twigs of medicinal plants.

Once ready, they looked at the vaid. The vaid checked the consistency of the mixture and, on being satisfied, he mixed the paste with the spring water that had been specially brought from a remote hill.

They were ready. With his assistants helping him lift the king's head, the vaid brought the soupy concoction to the Swargadeo's lips.

But Jayadhwaj clenched his jaw tight and the liquid spilled from both sides of his mouth. The vaid panicked and sent his assistant to call Himabhas.

With the Prime Minister's help, the vaid forcibly opened Jayadhwaj's mouth and made sure the medicine was consumed. The king coughed and then was quiet.

The medicine had been administered. Now, all they could do was wait.

Meanwhile, on the rooftop, the kingdom's priest performed a special yagna, and the chanting of mantras continued throughout the night.

But, by the next morning, the king was pronounced dead. The palace sank into further sorrow. Official mourners walked the streets of the capital, beating their chests and wailing in grief.

Tragically, the king's funeral wasn't a grand affair as it should have been. The Mughals had left behind financial advisors to control the Ahom's treasuries, and these men heartlessly blocked the sanction that Himabhas proposed. Finally, the prime minister had to borrow money from the other Ahom leaders, and the last rites were performed in a subdued manner. Less than fifty people attended the funeral.

After cremation, the leaders of the Ahom court were called for an emergency meeting. They were told that there was an urgent matter that needed to be discussed. The king had not named an heir, so the kingdom didn't have a legitimate successor.

Himabhas presided over the meeting. Those present included Borphukan, Buragohain, Borgohain, six princes from minor kingdoms which were a part of the Ahom empire, including Chakradhwaj's, and Lachit. Lachit's order of expulsion from Jorhat was revoked by Himabhas with the support of senior members of the court. On one side, against the wall, sat three Mughal advisors.

As soon as everyone had settled, Himabhas began, 'As you know, the Swargadeo of the Ahom kingdom has passed away without naming an heir. Now, we need to select a new Swargadeo. Before I share what is on my mind, I would like to invite proposals from senior members of the Ahom court.'

Borphukan was the first to speak, 'I have always believed in fair competition. Let the worthiest win and wear the crown.'

Himabhas looked at the others. Everyone mumbled their agreement.

Himabhas said, 'In fact, we, the patra mantris, feel the same. There should be a competition among the princes of different provinces. As a rule, every prince will select a shield bearer and—'

Borgohain interrupted him, 'A shield bearer? Can you elaborate what you mean by this?'

He nodded and continued, 'Yes, I will. First, to become eligible, the shield bearer must publicly kill a crocodile, a wild bull or a rhino. After killing the animal, the shield bearers will use the hide of the dead animal on their prince's shield. Once all the princes have their shields covered, we will have a sword fight between the princes. The final winner will wear the crown and become the new Swargadeo of the Ahoms.'

The princes looked at one another. A silent communication seemed to pass between them before everyone said that they agreed to such a competition.

Himabhas clapped his palms together to draw everyone's attention and said, 'Good, it's settled then. As the first stage, the princes will have to register the names of their shield bearers who will kill the animal for them and bring the hide. These assistants will then stretch and affix the hides on the shields in our presence. Once all the shields are ready, the princes will fight it out in the Rang Ghar.'

One by one, the princes mentioned the names of their closest allies and these were duly noted down by the court's clerk. When it was Chakradhwaj's turn, he looked at Lachit and said, 'I select Lachit Borphukan as my shield bearer.'

Lachit's chest swelled with pride. He bowed towards Chakradhwaj.

The meeting was over. The Mughal advisors had stayed silent, justifiably so, because their mandate was only to observe and send a report, besides making sure half the king's earnings were sent to Agra.

After the meeting, Chakradhwaj and Lachit walked outside the court. As they crossed the elaborate fountains and landscaped gardens, Lachit said, 'I'm very excited about this, Chakradhwaj. I'm certain, you will win.'

Chakradhwaj stopped and placed a hand on his best friend's shoulders and said, 'Thank you, brother. And I'm very sorry for what happened to Princess Padmini.'

Lachit nodded.

'I wish we had a chance to rescue her,' Chakradhwaj added.

Lachit's eyes brimmed, 'I tried. I had a chance. But ... but ...'

Chakradhwaj's eyebrows raised, 'But ... but what?'

He inhaled deeply and said, 'She refused to come with me.'

'What? Refused?'

'She wanted to honour the word given by the king of Ahoms ... our king and her father.'

'Hmm ...'

'Once you become the king, Chakradhwaj, we will rescue Padmini and throw these Mughals out of Jorhat.'

'That's what we will do, Lachit, I promise. Because only then can I stop being a puppet and become the real king.'

They were quiet for a few seconds before Lachit stamped his foot in anger.

'Save your anger, brother. I will need you soon. Have you decided which animal you will kill for the hide?'

Lachit smiled and said, 'Yes, the rhino.'

'The rhino will be toughest to kill, Lachit. Why not a bull? I know you won't touch a crocodile.'

He smiled, 'Because I want the thickest hide for my prince's shield.'

Chakradhwaj hugged him.

Unlike Lachit, all the shield bearers had selected either a crocodile or a wild bull. The princes were uncomfortable with the pair of Chakradhwaj and Lachit because they knew the potential of this combination. But they hoped for something to go wrong when the day arrived. They were not aware at the time that the tables were about to turn against Chakradhwaj.

After bidding farewell to Chakradhwaj, Lachit went to the jungle. Over the next two days, he wandered in search of a large rhino so that he could have the strongest hide for the prince's shield.

On the third morning, deep in the jungle, Lachit finally found a huge rhino. He followed it for a couple of hours and observed the animal's behaviour. It was a beautiful autumn day with crisp sun and cool wind.

He selected a perfect spot where the rhino was expected to arrive, and after readying his bow and arrow for the kill, he laid in wait. Ten minutes later, on the way to a water source, the rhino arrived at the location.

Lachit knew that there were very few soft spots on the body of a rhino that an arrow could penetrate. His strategy, therefore, was to first shock the animal with a painful strike by a poisoned-tip arrow, then get close to him by taking advantage of its lack of mobility for a few seconds and finally hit him with a spear on the same spot.

The setting was perfect. The visibility was good, and the animal was quietly walking towards him. Before pulling the string of his bow, Lachit factored in the slight wind which was blowing from the west and calculated his arrow's trajectory. Then he took a deep breath. He was ready. The spear was kept right next to him for the next stage of the attack.

The rhino reached the spot that Lachit had anticipated and stopped. Then, it turned its head and looked in the direction where Lachit was hiding in the bushes. Its eyes landed exactly where Lachit was. It was as if the animal could see Lachit through the thick obstruction of foliage.

Lachit's sixth sense raised a red flag, and a voice in his head said, '*There is something odd in the behaviour of this rhino, Lachit.*'

Riding the wave of uncertainty that followed, just as Lachit was about to release the arrow, he saw a baby rhino approach the adult rhino. Lachit stopped and slowly brought the string back to its position. He then removed the arrow and started to watch, transfixed, as the baby began to suckle milk.

The baby's and the mother's faces looked peaceful. The more he watched them, the more profound effect it had on him. Lachit realized the grave mistake he was about to commit. He stepped out of his hiding position.

The rhino spotted Lachit and, in the next moment, began to charge towards him. As it made the dash to strike Lachit with its horn, the rhino looked ferocious. Everything was happening so quickly that Lachit was unable to move.

A few feet from Lachit, the rhino stopped, its hoofs dragging through the moist ground. Lachit was too dazed to even move as the rhino's horn came to a stop just an inch from his forehead.

Their eyes locked. Time stood still. Then, the rhino exhaled deeply, turned and walked away. Lachit sighed in relief. His life had been spared, just as he had spared the animal's life. Was it an act of reciprocation? Perhaps, it was.

Standing alone in the jungle and deeply moved by this experience, Lachit decided not to kill another rhino and whispered, 'Prince Chakradhwaj, I will be your shield. I will protect you with my body and my skin. Before any harm comes to you, it will first come to me.'

Lachit mounted his horse and rode to the palace to tell Prince Chakradhwaj about his decision.

After listening to Lachit patiently, Chakradhwaj said, 'My brother, this is not correct. I wouldn't allow this to happen. I want you to fight alongside me as you have always been. I can never take shelter behind your body to fight.'

'Chakradhwaj, my prince, trust me. Place your legs on my shoulders and join the competition. I want you to win and make us free.'

He hesitated for a moment, but seeing the larger picture, he nodded, 'After I win, I would like to see you as the new borphukan and naubaicha phukan.'

Lachit smiled. The pact had been made.

CHAPTER 7

———〜〜———

At the Ahom palace the next morning, the court was in progress. Himabhas was chairing the session, and besides Borphukan, Buragohain, Borgohain and Lachit, all the princes were present. The Mughal advisors were in attendance as well, silently observing the proceedings.

Himabhas said, 'Today is an important day as we are here to take a decision regarding the selection of our new Swargadeo. Let me first apprise you about the status of the shields. All the nominated shield bearers of the princes have killed the chosen animals and presented the hides, except for Lachit.'

Heads turned to first look at Chakradhwaj and then at Lachit. A few princes couldn't stop smirking. If Chakradhwaj were disqualified, their chances of winning the competition and ascending the throne would become significantly higher.

The prime minister continued, 'Chakradhwaj, do you wish to select someone else in Lachit's place? We can give you one more day.'

Chakradhwaj said, 'No, I don't want anyone else.' He turned towards Lachit and asked, 'Do you want to say something?'

Lachit stood up, his face grave as he spoke in a deep voice, 'Prime Minster Himabhas, while it is right that I have not killed an animal, I would like to offer myself as Prince Chakradhwaj's shield, so that he can place his feet on my shoulders and fight.'

A few princes shot up to their feet and said, 'This is illegal, this can't be allowed.'

'Be quiet,' Himabhas said, his voice raised.

The princes sat down.

Lachit continued, 'I beg to differ with the princes. Instead of an animal's skin, I'm offering my own skin for the protection of the prince. How can this be illegal?'

Himabhas thought for a few seconds before speaking, 'I think Lachit is right, but let me consult the leaders of the court. Borphukan, let's begin with you. What do you think?'

Borphukan first looked at Lachit before facing Himabhas as he said, 'Lachit is my son, but, as the Borphukan, I'll remain unbiased. In my opinion, Lachit's proposal is different, but it is not illegal.'

'Gohains?'

Both of them, one after the other, said that what Lachit had proposed was not illegal.

'It's settled then. The competition will be held at the Rang Ghar after a month. May the best one win.'

The princes looked at the Prime Minster and, although they didn't say anything, their expressions betrayed what was in their minds. Then, a few of them turned to look at the Mughal advisors. The elders of the court missed noticing the silent communication that passed between them.

———•———

It was evening. At the prime minister's residence, Borphukan and Himabhas were sitting in the courtyard. The ambience was relaxed, and they were drinking luk-lao.

Himabhas was speaking. 'I was impressed by what Lachit said today. His loyalty for Chakradhwaj is beyond words.'

Borphukan nodded, 'I agree.'

'Loyalty apart, he is also exceptionally brave. The way he won the competition, I had never seen anything like that in my life.'

'Yashodhara and I are very proud of our son and we pray he takes over my position as the Borphukan of the Ahom army one day. I think he is ready.'

Himabhas said, 'I talk from experience, and I think your son is actually overqualified to become the Borphukan.'

Borpukhan looked up sharply, 'Overqualified? What do you mean, Himabhas?'

'Well, what I mean is … what I mean is … he is actually qualified to become the king.'

Borphukan got up to his feet and said, 'Prime Minister, I'm sorry, but I don't appreciate this kind of humour.'

'Sit down, Borphukan. This is not humour; it is the truth. Since Lachit has already defeated Prince Chakradhwaj in front of everyone, do you think the people of Ahom will be happy to see Chakradhwaj ascend the throne?'

Borphukan sat down and spoke after a few moments, 'But Lachit is my son, and we are not of royal blood. We aren't eligible to become kings.'

Himabhas smiled and said, 'You are right. That is how it was when the king was alive. But now, the king is dead, and, as the prime minister, I have the power to make this change.'

Borphukan's body language had transformed. He eyed him suspiciously and said, 'Why would you do that?'

Himabhas looked to his left and right before whispering, 'So that we get a more deserving king, who is efficient and brave enough to motivate everyone in the Ahom kingdom to throw the Mughals out.'

Borphukan stared at the prime minister for a few moments. Then, he got to his feet and said, 'I must leave now. I think you have had a lot of wine.'

Himabhas had not expected this, but he replied cheerfully, 'Good night, Borphukan.'

'Good night, Himabhas.'

After Borphukan was gone, a young girl walked to where he was seated and asked, 'Father, what did he say?'

'You heard every word, didn't you, Vedha?'

She smiled shyly and said, 'Yes, why shouldn't I, when it will impact my life more than anyone else's?'

Vedha, the beautiful sixteen-year-old daughter of Himabhas, was in love with Lachit. She had seen him only twice, but through her father and her father's spies, she had been following his achievements and movements for a long time. When Lachit had eloped with Padmini, she was devastated, but since the time Padmini was given away by her father to the Mughals and Lachit had returned to the capital, she was happy.

Vedha was an excellent singer, but as a person, unless she was surrounded by people close to her, she was shy.

Himabhas smiled and said, 'I'll try my best to make my daughter happy. I'm myself impressed by Lachit, and I'm convinced that he deserves the throne more than anyone else.'

———•———

Chakradhwaj had seen Vedha a few times and was smitten by her. After becoming the king, which he was sure was only a matter of time before it became reality, he had already decided that his first action would be to propose to her.

One part of the young prince wanted to meet her right then but the other, stronger part, had convinced him that he should first sit on the throne and then profess his love to her. He knew love at first sight always came with a risk. *What if she turned me down*—this thought had time and again made him anxious.

The morning after Himabhas had declared that the competition among the princes would be held after a month, Chakradhwaj and Lachit rode towards the jungle to practice sword fighting. The early morning fog was yet to dissipate and, with November just around the corner, the weather had turned nippy.

After selecting a spot on the banks of the Brahmaputra, both dismounted from their horses and left them open to graze. It was time to practice.

They had real hengdang swords in their hands and they fought with gusto. Chakradhwaj realized that Lachit was not in his best form. After an hour, when they were resting on the banks of the river, Chakradhwaj asked, 'You are not yourself today, Lachit. Something on your mind, brother?'

Lachit replied, 'No, I'm fine, it's just that … let's leave it.'

'I know what's on your mind, Lachit. I'm your best friend, closer to you than most people are to their own brothers.'

Lachit nodded but didn't say anything as Chakradhwaj continued, 'You are thinking about Padmini, aren't you?'

Lachit looked at him, his eyes moistening, 'How is she? I hope she is well. I can't sleep at night thinking of her.'

'One of our spies is on his way back here. He should arrive soon. We should know then.'

'I feel so helpless, Chakradhwaj. I hope they are treating her well.'

'We Ahoms have honoured every word of the treaty and we expect the same from the Mughals.'

They were silent for a few moments before Chakradhwaj said, 'Lachit, can I ask you for something?'

'Of course, everything is yours, Prince Chakradhwaj, including my life. Tell me, what can I do for you?'

'Do you know Vedha?'

'Vedha? You mean Himabhas's daughter?'

Chakradhwaj hesitated, 'Yes ... I have never talked to her, though I've seen her ... and I have heard she is a good singer.'

Lachit smiled, 'Got it! You don't have to say anything more.'

'No, I mean, yes, I like her, but she doesn't know it yet.'

'So, you go and tell her. She will be over the moon when she realizes that the soon-to-be king is in love with her.'

'But I don't want to face her right now. Once I'm the king, I will go and propose to her.'

Lachit got to his feet. He was surprised, 'What are you saying? Once you are the king, you will be the leader of the Ahom people. That's not the time to demand something like love. You need to do it now. Because if she wants to reject you, she can do it. Once you are the king, she will have no option but to say yes.'

'You mean ...'

'I mean, what are you worried about? You are the best in the Ahom kingdom. You are handsome, you are educated, you are brave and you are a prince, of royal blood.'

'Well, if you say so ...'

'Look, I will arrange a meeting in a day or two. Meet Vedha and tell her how you feel about her, okay?'

Chakradhwaj nodded.

'Come on, what are friends for? Pick up your sword now. Let's practice again.'

That evening, on their return to the capital, Lachit bid farewell to Chakradhwaj and rode towards the prime minister's house.

The guard escorted Lachit inside to a room where Himabhas was seated with two people. Lachit waited for the meeting to finish.

After the visitors had left, Himabhas turned towards Lachit and said, 'Lachit, what a surprise to see you. What is so urgent that you want to see me at my house? Couldn't this have waited till tomorrow morning?'

Lachit conveyed his protest with a smile, well aware that if Himabhas hadn't wanted to meet him, Himabhas could have asked the guard and sent him away. 'Prime Minister Himabhas, thank you for meeting me. I assure you, this is an important matter.'

'Of course, it is. Tell me, what can I do for you?'

'Well, thank you,' he hesitated, momentarily worried if he was doing the right thing, but found the confidence to continue, 'I am here as Prince Chakradhwaj's friend.'

'Prince Chakradhwaj has sent you?'

'No, no … I mean, I have come here to speak to you about something important … something that he can't tell you in person.'

Himabhas crossed his arms. It was an awkward situation and he had no idea about the reason for Lachit's visit. He had a premonition though, that he was about to be confronted with something that wasn't good for him. 'I'm waiting. After you finish saying what you are here for, I have something to say to you too. In fact, I've already told your father.'

'Oh!' This was a welcome window to buy some time before Lachit was mentally ready to speak his mind, so he said, 'No, how is that possible? You are elder to me, so you should speak first.'

'But you have come to meet me, so it's only right that you speak first.'

Lachit realized he had been cornered, so he started, 'Prime Minister Himabhas, I have come here to share something that is not just good for your family but is in the best interest of the entire Ahom kingdom.'

'Yes, go on.'

'The fact is that Chakradhwaj loves your daughter Vedha.'

'What?' Himabhas was shocked.

Taking his shock as a pleasant reaction, Lachit continued, 'Isn't this the best alliance ever? Chakradhwaj will soon be the king, and your daughter, Vedha, will be the queen.'

Himabhas placed his head between his palms and pressed it hard.

Lachit smiled, 'I can totally understand your feelings. It will take some time to sink in. Please tell Vedha how lucky she is.'

Himabhas looked up and said, 'Lachit, this is not right. You don't understand.'

It was Lachit's turn to be shocked now. 'What is not right? And what don't I understand?'

Himabhas placed a hand on Lachit's shoulder and said, 'Listen to me carefully, young man. Chakradhwaj is not the right person for the Ahom throne.'

Lachit shook his hand off and spoke, his voice higher, 'What are you saying? How can you say this even before the competition? I will make sure he wins.'

'I know you will, Lachit. But the people of Ahom will not accept him as the king because you had defeated him in the previous competition and Padmini had garlanded you.'

'That was a thousand years ago, Prime Minister, when Padmini was the princess, our kingdom had a king and we were *free*.'

Lachit had spoken very loudly. But he felt no guilt as he looked at Himabhas.

'Lachit, our kingdom needs a capable king, and if you trust my experience in life, you are more suitable for the throne than Chakradhwaj. That is what I told your father as well.'

Lachit kept quiet, his eyes darting in all directions, avoiding Himabhas.

Himabhas continued, 'Lachit, the fact is, Vedha likes you.'

'What? But that's not right. I'm in love with Padmini.'

'She knows that too, but Padmini is gone …'

'I had never thought I would say this, but I think you have left me with no choice. You are … you are …'

'Lachit, I understand you are angry. But matters of the heart can't be decided by muscles or anger. I respect your emotions. If you feel what you think is right, I'm prepared to support you.'

Lachit asked, incredulous, 'Really?'

'Yes. But you will have to do something for me.'

'What is it?'

'I can't tell Vedha what you have told me. Therefore, I want you to go and give this news to her. She loves you, and it is only fair that *you* break her heart.'

Lachit got to his feet, bowed and walked away.

———◦———

The next morning, Lachit and Vedha were seated on a bench in a garden. She had tears in her eyes. Lachit had told her that he couldn't love her because he was in love with Padmini and could not love any other woman in this life.

'I'm sorry, Vedha. You are a very beautiful and talented girl.'

She didn't reply, and Lachit realized it was time to bring in Chakradhwaj. He smiled and said, 'Prince Chakradhwaj really loves you, Vedha.'

She looked up and searched his face but again didn't say anything.

His smile widened, 'You should see him when he talks about you. I've known him for such a long time and I'm his best friend, but I have never seen him behave like this.'

'But, but … I love you, Lachit. Only *you*.'

Lachit looked away. This was not going well and he knew he had to come up with something quickly.

After a few moments, he said, 'Please understand, I love someone else, and that love can never die. I'm sorry, but I don't love you.'

She gasped.

He continued, 'But, as I said, Chakradhwaj loves you. He loves you with all his heart and, as a woman, if you accept his proposal, your life will be full of love and happiness.'

She stayed silent, her tears flowing freely.

After a couple of minutes, Lachit said, 'You said you love me, right?'

She nodded, looking at him with hope in her eyes.

'If you love me so much, you will have to sacrifice your love because I'm asking you to do it.'

She took a deep breath, wiped her tears and said, 'Because this is not my decision but the decision of the man I love, I agree.'

Lachit took a deep breath of relief as soon as she was gone.

———•———

In Agra, Padmini was a part of the harem but, being very young, Emperor Aurangzeb hadn't touched her so far. She was being taught how to behave like a royal Mughal woman. Since the king was old, it was expected that he would present her as a gift to his most capable son who would ascend the throne.

This was a new world for Padmini. Everything was different: the food, the language, the music, the prayers, the palaces, the gardens and even the horses, dogs and cats.

She missed Lachit and dreamt of a day when her hero would come and rescue her, as he had from the palace in Jorhat. What an adventure it had been! She remembered what Tapani had said, 'Your prince will come one day and take you to a beautiful place.'

But her more practical side knew that this was impossible as the wealth and power of the Ahom kingdom were depleting. Over time, she feared that the entire kingdom would be subsumed by the Mughals. And yet, she couldn't completely get rid of her thoughts of freedom and the restoration of the Ahom flag over Jorhat.

At night, after everyone had gone to sleep, she wrote letters to Lachit. In these, she talked about how much she missed him. But she didn't send any of these letters to him. If the spy network of the Mughals read any one of them, her loyalty would be questioned and she would be beheaded. The Mughals would impose a fine on the Ahoms too, or just go on a rampage, killing innocent citizens of the country of her birth. All she could do, therefore, was wait. But, as time elapsed, her helplessness multiplied.

Aurangzeb's favourite son, Muhammed Akbar, whom he fondly called Bahaadur, was smitten with Padmini. He had only seen glimpses of her on a few occasions as she lived in the zenana, where men were not allowed.

Bahaadur secretly commissioned a female artist to make a painting of Padmini and bring it to him when it was ready. The artist's job was not easy as she had to complete the painting without Padmini or anyone knowing about it. So, she employed a simple and practical method. While she kept the life-sized canvas at her home, she sketched parts of Padmini's body on small pieces of silk and smuggled them out of the zenana. Bit by bit, while Prince Bahaadur was busy with his campaign in the Deccan, she completed the painting.

Upon his return, after the Mughals had succeeded in crushing a local rebellion, one evening, the prince called the artist to his personal chamber. A few hours later, she arrived with a covered, life-sized wooden board that was carried by her assistant.

Bahaadur dismissed her assistant and his own two guards from the chamber and said, 'Show me what you have got.'

The woman bowed and said, 'My great prince, before I show you the painting, I must tell you that Padmini is so beautiful that no artist in the world can capture her beauty and charm in one painting. I have tried my best.'

The Prince wasn't able to contain his excitement and ordered, 'Show me *now*.'

The woman pulled the silk cloth, which came off in one smooth motion.

Prince Bahaadur stood up.

Princess Padmini was right in front of him, her eyes directed at him, a hint of a smile on her magnetic and achingly beautiful face. It was like an ocean of mystery, her eyes a lighthouse for lost souls and her lips slightly parted, as if she was about to break into a melodious song.

'Subhanallah!' exclaimed Bahaadur and signalled the artist to leave him and his painting alone. The woman bowed and left.

Bahaadur took a couple of steps forward until his face was a few inches from Padmini's. He smiled and whispered, 'You are the most beautiful woman in the world, Princess Padmini of Ahom. I love you.'

His face moved closer to Padmini's lips to kiss them when he heard a voice from behind. Alarmed, he turned.

It was his mother, Dilras Bano Begam. She glanced at the painting, scrutinized her son from top to bottom and asked, 'What is all this?'

Bahaadur stammered, 'Queen mother, this is … this is …'

She raised her hand to silence him. 'I know who this is. What surprises me is that if you like her so much, why this secrecy? Why haven't you spoken to the emperor and me?'

'I want to, Queen mother. But she is new here, and I don't want to rush. I have been told that she is adapting well to our culture.'

Bano Begam smiled and said, 'I never knew my son would fall in love with a foreign princess one day.'

'She is no longer foreign. She is now one of our own.'

'Do you really love her?'

He was embarrassed, but he managed to speak, his eyes avoiding looking directly at his mother's face, 'Yes, I do.'

She continued, 'Don't worry, your choice is excellent. She is an Ahom royal. Her people are courageous and have a lot of self-respect. I will keep an eye on her for you from today, okay?'

He nodded.

'Now, smile.'

Prince Bahaadur looked at his mother and smiled.

Vedha stuck to the promise she had given Lachit and agreed to meet Prince Chakradhwaj after a few days. The meeting was arranged for ten in the morning by Himabhas at the Rang Ghar.

Chakradhwaj arrived there at nine, accompanied by Lachit. Without the presence of people and the colourful flags all around, the amphitheatre looked greyer than it really was. There was no charging buffalo or escaping pigeons today. There was no roar of anticipation or the collective gasp of shock. The October wind on the skin was cool and the sun was hidden under a thick blanket of clouds.

Chakradhwaj smiled widely at Lachit and began to run around the arena with childlike enthusiasm. *Perhaps, he wanted to reduce his excitement before Vedha arrived*, Lachit thought, *so that he didn't come across as too eager.* Perhaps, no such thought crossed his mind and he was just behaving as any young man in love would.

Standing at the same spot, Lachit watched him, a gentle smile on his lips. He was happy for Chakradhwaj, the future king, who was about to fulfil his desire to be united with his beloved, Vedha. The Ahom kingdom was just days away from getting a worthy king and a queen.

'Vedha!' Chakradhwaj shouted as he ran.

After half an hour, he stopped next to Lachit and, trying to catch his breath, his torso bent, he said, 'Why is she late?'

Lachit placed his hands on his shoulders, bent down to come to his level and said, 'It's still not ten, Prince.'

'Then make it ten, Lachit. I can't wait any longer.'

Lachit laughed heartily and stepped away from him. Then, with his hands extended ahead of him, as if he was addressing people in the stadium, he began to speak loudly, 'Dear people of Ahom, your future king, Prince Chakradhwaj, is in love.'

His voice echoed, appearing to bounce off the stone steps.

Lachit turned towards Chakradhwaj, 'Did you hear that?'

It was now Chakradhwaj's turn to add to the drama, 'The people of Ahom, I thank you on behalf of my beloved and me. Thank you, thank you and thank you!'

Lowering his voice, Chakradhwaj asked Lachit, 'Now what?'

'Look at you! You are sweating through every pore of your body. What will the future queen think?' Lachit's voice had a playful admonishment to it.

'Right.'

'Go behind the royal gallery. I've got two people waiting for you. They will take care of you.'

Chakradhwaj winked, 'What would I do without you, Lachit?'

With that, he moved away. Lachit inhaled deeply. Everything was going as planned. He hoped Vedha played her part well.

A few minutes later, Vedha arrived with two female companions. They were the same age as Vedha, so Lachit presumed they were her friends.

She faced Lachit and said, 'I am ready.'

Lachit looked at her face closely. Her eyes were red and her face appeared to be a bit swollen. When she noticed

Lachit scrutinizing her closely, she smiled and repeated, 'I'm ready.'

'Ready for what?' Lachit asked without thinking and silently cursed himself.

'Ready to obey your command.'

He extended his hand and pulled her to one side, so that they were out of earshot of her two young friends.

Lachit whispered, his tone annoyed, 'Vedha. It's not anyone's command. You deserve the prince, as much as he deserves you. He's madly in love with you. With you by his side, the Ahoms will have a stable state.'

She freed her arm and said, 'Okay, let me rephrase then. I'm ready to sacrifice my life to make the kingdom stable.'

Lachit's face was a mix of disappointment and sadness. He tried again, 'Fine, let me do it your way. As the man you love, I command you to love Chakradhwaj and get married to him.'

She smiled and said, 'As a woman who can only love you, I accept your command.'

With that, she turned and walked to her friends.

Lachit spotted Chakradhwaj walking towards them. He had washed and looked fresh. As he neared, his perfume enveloped them. His eyes were constantly on Vedha and he was smiling ear to ear. Lachit moved away and so did Vedha's friends.

Chakradhwaj came to a stop near Vedha. Lachit sat on the lowermost step of the amphitheatre, a little distance away, and watched them from the corner of his eye.

He saw Chakradhwaj say something, but Lachit's eyes were on Vedha. With halted breath, he saw her smile and nod her head. *Had Chakradhwaj professed his love and she nodded? Or had Chakradhwaj commented about the pleasant weather and she'd nodded?* Lachit had no way of knowing.

He watched their lips move. Chakradhwaj spoke more enthusiastically than Vedha, but that was expected in their initial courtship. After a few minutes, Chakradhwaj extended his hands to her. She seemed to hesitate but then took his hands into hers. He pulled her closer.

Lachit watched Chakradhwaj bend his head down and rest the top of his forehead on hers. They looked like people in love, except that Lachit knew that they weren't—at least, Vedha wasn't.

Chakradhwaj then placed his hands on her waist and pulled her even closer. She cooperated, her eyes on Chakradhwaj as he began to sway his body in an impromptu dance. On seeing them, Lachit's thoughts turned towards Padmini. He knew that her spirit was right here with him, but would he ever be able to free her body? He turned his head away from Chakradhwaj and Vedha as tears welled in his eyes.

When he turned back to look at them, Chakradhwaj and Vedha were still dancing, but his back was towards Lachit, and her eyes were directly on him. Vedha's cheeks were tear-stained. This was not going well.

Lachit admonished her with his gestures and she brought her hand to her face to wipe her tears. The next second, Chakradhwaj pulled away so that she faced him. Then, he turned to look towards Lachit.

Chakradhwaj's expression had changed. Lachit looked away.

After some time, Vedha left with her friends and Chakradhwaj approached Lachit. Lachit got to his feet. Something was not right.

Chakradhwaj said, 'Brother, Vedha has said yes.'

Lachit smiled as widely as his face allowed him; he was genuinely happy, 'That is such terrific news.'

Chakradhwaj hugged him.

After a few moments, he added, 'But …'

Lachit was alarmed, 'But what?'

'She appeared to be guarded. I think … I think she is hiding something from me.'

'Is she? I don't think so. Girls are different. Maybe she is just a bit overwhelmed by the future king proposing to her. Think about that.'

'I don't think that is the case, but I trust your judgement more than mine, Lachit.'

Lachit said, 'Thank you! For me, your life is more important than my own.'

Chakradhwaj hugged him again. Lachit felt awkward as he smelled Vedha in his arms.

———•———

Prince Chakradhwaj and Vedha's wedding was finalized. It was three days after she had said yes. The palace drummers went around the town announcing the good news. As a royal prince and a probable king, Chakradhwaj had considerable clout.

The other princes of the kingdom were unhappy with the developments. There were two reasons for this. One, Chakradhwaj's proposal to allow Lachit to become his shield was accepted by the court. And second, the prime minister's daughter, Vedha, was days away from getting married to Chakradhwaj.

The six remaining princes decided to call for a secret meeting. The venue had on be carefully selected. After internal discussions, they zeroed in to an old ruin that once belonged to the Ahom royal family but was now dilapidated due to disuse and age. It was located in a remote part of the jungle.

Secrecy was of utmost importance as their agenda was to discuss ways to break the duo of Chakradhwaj and Lachit and, if possible, derail Chakradhwaj's plans to marry the most beautiful girl in the kingdom, Vedha.

The tallest and the fieriest of them all was called Prince Chung Mung. After all the others had settled, he began, 'My dear princes, welcome to this meeting. Our sole aim is to save the Ahom kingdom. This is not about us … this is about the people of Ahom and our rich and proud history.'

All the princes nodded and waited for more, as Chung Mung continued, 'This competition to select the next Swargadeo isn't fair. To me, everything looks pre-decided.'

One of the princes reacted angrily, 'That's right. And we can't just sit and watch, sucking our thumbs.'

Chung Mung raised his hand, 'Save that anger for later, Prince. Right now, all of us need to put our heads together and think.'

They nodded again. The princes were accompanied by a few guards and servants. The servants began serving wine.

Chung Mung continued, 'This competition is being organized by the prime minister and one of the competitors is getting married to his daughter. Now, you tell me, dear princes, why would the prime minister not make sure that his son-in-law wins and becomes the king?'

A prince said, 'Where have the fairness and encouragement of talent of Ahoms gone?'

Another added, 'The question is, when we know the result even before the competition begins, why should we participate? Just to lose?'

The discussions continued, and as the time progressed, everyone realized that they were all on the same page—this competition was rigged!

With time, as they kept on drinking, their motives started to get increasingly dangerous.

One prince declared, 'The time has come to stop this nonsense.'

Another asserted, 'If they think we can do nothing, then, well, they are wrong.'

The anger and frustration continued to rise, and all the princes opened up.

'We have supporters who are loyal to us. Supporters who are tired of this cheap trickery of Ahom leadership.'

'I'm so angry that the Swargadeo gave up without even lifting his sword ...'

'And presented the princess to them.'

Chung Mung raised his hand and said, 'Princes, allow me to sum up. A man who can't protect the honour of his own daughter can't be someone whose policies we need to follow. He was a coward and a dishonest man, and so are his disciples and his favourite people. Yes, I'm talking about Himabhas, Chakradhwaj, Borphukan and Lachit. Now, the question is, what can we do?'

They were quiet for a few minutes, thinking.

Finally, Chung Mung said, 'I have a plan and I want to present it to you, my learned princes. Should I share it?'

They nodded.

Chung Mung took a deep breath and continued, 'Okay, here is what we could do. 'I know the chief of the Barman Karachi tribals. He lives high up in the mountains. I'll contact him. He's very popular, and other tribal leaders at the far end of our land listen to him. Let's ask for their support and attack Jorhat to throw Himabhas and his cheats away.'

The princes looked at one another. They had gone too far.

Prince Chung Mung, who had clearly emerged as the angriest and the leader of their resistance, said, 'I think it's time to take a decision now ... Those of you who want to be a part of this revolution, raise your hands.'

Two princes raised their hands, while three didn't.

'Fair enough. I respect your decisions. The three of you can now go back to the capital. You must honour the secrecy of our project, and we promise not to touch you when we take over the capital.'

The three princes nodded, wished them luck and left. The plan had been finalized and, in the days to come, the troubles of Ahom kingdom were about to multiply.

As soon as the princes had left, Chung Mung signalled his deputy to step closer to him. Then, he whispered in his ears, his voice dramatically high so that everyone present could hear, 'I don't want these princes to reach Jorhat. Kill them.'

CHAPTER 8

━━◦◦◦━━

A grand chak-long, spread over nine days, was planned to unite Vedha and Chakradhwaj in marriage, and every day, as advised by the Deodhai priests, the age-old holy customs were followed.

Chakradhwaj's family had travelled from Naigaon. Besides his father and mother, his sister had also arrived. Other members of the royal court of Naigaon and a few noblemen were present, too.

Chakradhwaj's father was a righteous king who ruled the minor kingdom of Naigaon efficiently. He was also one of the closest aides to the former Swargadeo. Like Chakradhwaj, he was tall and well-built. In contrast, Chakradhwaj's mother was short and led a very quiet life in the shadow of her husband. But Chakradhwaj's sister,

Yutika, was different. Although she was fourteen years old, she still had the curiosity of a little child.

All through the marriage rituals, Yutika was seen running around, dancing, singing and encouraging everyone to participate enthusiastically. Her cheerful presence added to the charm of the festivities. Everyone was eager to talk to her and listen to her sing. Wherever she went, she was quickly surrounded by relatives, friends and well-wishers.

On the third day, the ceremony of pani-tola took place. Women from the bride's and bridegroom's households left for the Brahmaputra early in the morning and were back with freshwater before sunrise. For Vedha, this ceremony was one more step closer to the wedding day. She had accepted Chakradhwaj's proposal on the orders of Lachit but she still felt torn. As the women bathed her with the cold freshwater from the river, she let her tears flow. No one noticed her pain.

The ceremonies continued. On the ninth day, Chakradhwaj visited the bride's house wearing his finest suti sula and suria, a bejewelled safa resting on his head. Apart from his family, he was accompanied by Lachit.

Chakradhwaj sat in front of the one hundred and one lamps of clay that had carefully been arranged in six concentric circles. Confident as a man prepared to be married to the woman he loved with all his heart, the prince looked imposing. Lachit was proud of him.

The lamps were placed on a bed adorned with colourful rangoli patterns and as everyone waited, the priest chanted mantras.

It was finally time for the bride to arrive. When Vedha was escorted inside, not just Chakradhwaj's heart, but everyone's heart stopped beating for a few seconds. Wearing a pink-coloured riha and a mekhela chador made from the finest quality Muga silk, she looked stunning. Lachit looked away, fearful of prolonged eye contact.

Vedha kept her eyes downcast and stopped next to Chakradhwaj. According to the custom, the priest extended a tray on which a hengdang was kept. Then, he signalled to her to lift it and hand it over to her future husband.

As she did so, the priest chanted mantras in Ahom. Everyone present had an expression of contentment on their faces.

The priest simplified the relevance of the custom for everyone, 'Vedha has presented the hengdang to Prince Chakradhwaj and she agrees that he can now protect her and her family.'

Chakradhwaj bowed and smiled, 'Thank you, Vedha. I will protect your honour and your family's honour till the last drop of blood in my body is shed.'

Now, it was her turn to present the kavac-kapor to the prince. He accepted this and looked at it closely, before saying, 'I love the patterns in this, and I'll always keep it close to me, Vedha.'

The priest then began the ancestor worship rituals as he explained who their ancestors were and what they had accomplished in their lives.

In the end, the priest said, 'Now, the ancestors, as part of the supreme God, are showering their blessings on the new couple.'

Prince Chakradhwaj and Vedha bowed in respect. Then, they sought the blessings of Chakradhwaj's parents and Himabhas. Yutika joked that they should ask for her blessings too. All laughed heartily.

With this, the ceremony was over and everyone rejoiced. Food was served to all, and the guests were entertained by musical performances.

Chakradhwaj and Vedha were left by themselves, as others were busy eating, dancing or chatting. Under the glow of the evening lamps, Vedha looked stunning.

Chakradhwaj squeezed her palm. She looked up, alarmed, but a moment later, smiled.

He whispered, 'You look beautiful, Vedha. My Vedha.'

She nodded.

'I promise to keep you happy, sweetheart.'

She nodded again.

'Why don't you say something?'

From behind, he heard Lachit's voice greeting them, 'Congratulations to both of you!'

He came and stood before them.

Chakradhwaj was on his feet, 'Thank you, brother.'

They hugged each other.

Then Lachit addressed Vedha, 'Congratulations, Vedha.' She didn't reply nor look in his direction.

Chakradhwaj was annoyed, 'Vedha, Lachit is wishing you.'

'Oh, thank you,' she said, looking up at him as if breaking out of a trance.

Chakradhwaj's forehead creased. He seemed to get the same uncomfortable feeling once again that he had got at the Rang Ghar when he had proposed to Vedha.

But the creases vanished as he smiled and said, 'Lachit, why don't you eat?'

'I've already eaten, Prince. It's time for me to leave now. Congratulations to both of you once again.'

After he was gone, Chakradhwaj said, 'He was behaving in an odd way, don't you think, Vedha?'

'What can I say? He is your friend. I don't know him at all,' she replied.

———•———

Meanwhile, the rebel princes had convinced the Barman Kacharis that they needed to lay claim to the Ahom throne. The Barman Kacharis had sent emissaries to the Nagas, the Chutias and others.

All dissidents had combined, and their collective army was larger than the Ahom's standing army. It was time to choose the leader of their revolution.

In a meeting in the mountains, the leader was elected by the tribal elders and it was none other than Prince Chung Mung.

Chung Mung got up and bowed before the collective war council, raised his spear and said, 'I thank the council for electing me as the leader. Along with the brave tribals of the Ahom kingdom, I give you my word that I will rid Jorhat of the weak and corrupt people who have played with our honour. Victory to the Ahom tribals!'

All present raised their weapons and repeated, 'Victory to the Ahom tribals!'

At this moment, two guards brought in a man who was trembling with fear.

One of the guards said, 'This is an Ahom spy. We found him hiding in the tree. He has heard everything.'

Chung Mung got up, his eyes like burning embers, and approached the spy. 'You work for the Ahoms?'

He nodded, saliva dripping from his mouth and whispered, 'I'm sorry, I can work for you if you want.'

Chung Mung turned and spoke to everyone present, 'This is a typical Ahom man from Jorhat. He's ready to trade his honour and switch sides.'

Chung Mung asked the spy, 'Do any of you Ahom city people have a spine?'

The spy mumbled, 'I'm sorry, I didn't mean that.'

'I think we need to find out.'

With that, Chung Mung lifted him and threw him on the ground. He brought his spear down on him with full force, piercing his body. The man screamed in pain. Chung Mung pulled the spear out of his body and kept repeating the act of piercing and pulling for a long time, even after the spy had died.

Finally, he looked up from the mess at his feet and said, smiling, 'I knew they didn't have a spine but look at this mess. I think they don't even have a bone in their bodies.'

Everyone was quiet, and Chung Mung roared, 'Victory to the Ahom tribals!'

All present shouted back, 'Victory to the Ahom tribals!'

The dissidents had united and were ready with a fierce leader at the helm. The future of the Ahom kingdom had been decided.

———•———

The rebels didn't know that the spy they had caught and killed had not been alone. He had a companion in another tree, who was better hidden, and he had seen and heard everything, including the cold-blooded murder of his colleague.

By the time the meeting of the rebels was over, it was dawn. The spy waited for a few hours, and when he was sure that the enemies of the Ahom kingdom had gone, he cautiously climbed down the tree and started to make his way to Jorhat. His body was shaking with fear and he jumped at the slightest of sounds.

He arrived in Jorhat late at night and went straight to Borphukan's palace.

He told the guard at the gate, 'I have an important message for Borphukan.'

The guard said, 'I'm sorry, but you will have to wait till the morning.'

He folded his hands and with teary eyes, said, 'I beg you. It's urgent.'

The guard made a face, asked him to wait and went inside.

A few minutes later, a senior guard walked up to him and enquired, 'Yes?'

'I'm here to give an important piece of information to Borphukan. I can't give it to anyone else, not even to my boss, because there is very little time and it is about the security of the Ahom state.'

The senior guard replied, 'Son, meeting Borphukan is not possible. The only threat we have is from the Mughals, and they are already on our side. So, whatever you think is a security threat, isn't one.'

The spy stepped back and started to shout, 'Borphukan, there's another attack coming on Jorhat. Borphukan …'

The guards opened the gate and ran towards him. One of them jumped on him. They rolled around until the guard placed his palm on the spy's mouth and stopped his shouting. The spy bit into the guard's palm, who yelled in pain.

Lachit was strolling on the terrace. Hearing the commotion, he looked down from the parapet and asked, 'Hey, what's happening?'

He ran downstairs and came upon the guard who stood with a bleeding hand and a man whose clothes were torn and soiled and who looked at him with eyes wide with fear.

The senior guard arrived with a jug of water.

Lachit asked, 'Who is this?'

The senior guard handed over the jug to the bleeding guard and said, 'Lachit, he's a wayward person. He is saying Jorhat is about to be attacked.'

Lachit sat down on his hunches next to the fallen man. Just a few weeks before, the king had ignored Lachit's warning.

He helped him sit up. Then, he said, 'You don't have to be afraid. Tell us, who are you?'

'I'm a spy. My job is to comb through the jungles and monitor what the remote tribals are up to.'

'Go on.'

'Last night, up in the mountains, where the Barman Kacharis live … I was there with my partner. There was a big meeting, very secret, attended by a lot of tribals from different areas. Prince Chung Mung was there as well. They have made him the leader. After two days, they will attack Jorhat from two sides, from the main gates and from the riverside. They want to kill you, kill the borphukan, the prime minister and Prince Chakradhwaj. They killed my partner in front of my eyes.'

With this, he broke down.

Lachit said, 'You are very brave. What is your name?'

He replied, 'Lepi Run.'

'Okay, Lepi, you get washed up and meet me inside. I'll wake up Borphukan too. Tell us everything you saw and heard. And …' He paused, placed his hand on his shoulder and said, 'Thank you.'

After that, signalling to the guards, Lachit walked inside the palace, his eyes narrowed and forehead wrinkled.

Over the next hour, Borphukan and Lachit heard the man out completely and made a plan. They sent him away after paying him with a few gold coins. The spy had tears of gratitude in his eyes.

It was three in the morning. Borphukan sent messengers in all directions for an emergency meeting in the next hour in the main hall of the palace.

Then, as the father and son climbed mounted their horses, they bid farewell to Yashodhara, who had just woken up.

——•——

Within the hour, Himabhas, Prince Chakradhwaj, Borphukan, the two Gohains and Lachit had arrived in the palace's courtroom. The three Mughal advisors had arrived too.

Himabhas welcomed all of them, saying, 'This emergency meeting has been called as one of our spies witnessed a revolt assembly against the Ahom kingdom in the mountains yesterday. He was hiding there with another spy, whose presence was discovered, and they murdered him. The attack is coming the day after tomorrow. I first need your quick reactions. Let's begin with Borphukan.'

One of the Mughal advisors interrupted him, 'I would like to speak first as this is a matter of state security.'

Everyone present was offended, but they swallowed their pride as the Mughal advisor continued, 'You need a better spy network. Two days of reaction time is too little for me to get help from the Mughal army or navy. Even with the fastest speed, it will take a minimum of twelve days for them to reach here from Cooch Behar.'

Everyone waited for him to continue but when he didn't, Himabhas said, 'Noted. Borphukan?'

Borphukan cleared his throat and said, 'The attack will come from two sides. We need to divide our forces accordingly. I propose Lachit defend from the riverside and Chakradhwaj from the main gates.'

Both Chakradhwaj and Lachit nodded.

Borgohain spoke, 'I think we should focus on the gates as the tribals only have a few ships and our walls are formidable.'

Borphukan said, 'We shouldn't take any chances. Our intelligence is real. They might have a lot of small boats.'

They were quiet for a few moments, after which Buragohain asked, 'Who's leading them?'

Himabhas replied, 'Prince Chung Mung.'

Buragohain said, 'I know Chung Mung well. I think we all do. Expect him to be barbaric and break every rule of warfare.' He turned towards Lachit and Chakradhwaj and continued, 'Lachit, Chakradhwaj, you both have spent a lot of time with him in gurukul. Correct me if I'm wrong.'

Chakradhwaj replied, 'You are right.'

Himabhas said, 'Okay, enough! Let's plan a strategy to defend our city.'

Borphukan said, 'Right, follow me to the sand model.'

They walked to the end of the hall, where a sand model had been prepared to replicate the main features of the walled Ahom capital of Jorhat.

The strategic meeting continued for two hours. After that, with duties assigned, everyone dispersed.

By dawn, Lachit and Chakradhwaj had addressed their troops and, immediately afterwards, the mobilization of cannons, bombs, swords, spears, shields, boats and other items started.

———•———

Two days later, when Chung Mung and his fighters arrived at the point of the river that washed the periphery of Jorhat's walls, it was deathly quiet. The time was five in the morning, just before sunrise, and the river water was placid due to the absence of an early morning wind.

Chung Mung was required to first lay in wait here. The other two princes were ready at the main gates with their fighters.

The tribal rebels had planned a three-stage attack strategy. In the first stage, in order to precipitate panic among the unsuspecting Ahom forces, the attack was staged at the main gates. The tribals knew that this would result in the defenders concentrating their forces and weapons at the gates.

Exactly one hour later, in stage two, Chung Mung would breach the wall next to the river and lead his men to attack the defenders from behind. While this was underway, in stage three, a second major attack was planned from the main gates. The overall aim of the strategy was to confuse their opponents and make sure that the defence imploded as they would never be certain where the enemy was.

On the other side of the wall, near the river, Lachit, from his hideout, saw the enemy's ships and boats arrive and anchor quietly. He immediately drew their positions on a piece of cloth and sent it to Chakradhwaj through a messenger.

At the main gates, Chakradhwaj had sent a spy ahead of the gates during daytime and, therefore, as soon as the enemies arrived in position to attack, the spy took a circuitous route to evade capture and sneaked back into Jorhat with all the information. Chakradhwaj smiled as this was a minor attack by the enemy. He made his own drawing on a piece of cloth and sent Lachit's messenger back to him with it.

Now, both knew the enemy's positions. The number of enemy soldiers didn't match what the spy from the jungle had said, which meant another attack could come at a later stage.

Chung Mung had no idea that his plan had been punctured even before he had the chance to shout '*Attack!*'

For him, the city of Jorhat was asleep behind the walls, and so far, he had not noticed any movement in the vicinity of the walls. As they waited, a slight wind picked up from the west.

Chung Mung's flotilla comprised around one hundred vessels. While ten were large ships with multiple decks and several sails, the other ninety were smaller boats with just one deck and two sails. The large ships were positioned in the centre and the smaller ships were on their three sides— the front, port and starboard.

In the large ships, Chung Mung's oarsmen were ready in the lower decks to start rowing at a moment's notice, and on the main deck, his sailors were standing by to unfurl the sails. For the navigation and propulsion of his vessels, he had the sufficient manpower, and soon, he knew, the wind force would suitably increase to fill the sails.

Fifteen minutes before the scheduled time of attack, one of Chung Mung's lookouts, who was stationed in the foremost boat, noticed one boat approaching them. He quickly sent a smaller vessel towards Chung Mung's ship as a warning and waited, his arrow trained at the approaching boat.

The boat was a kayak, and as it neared, he saw that there was just one man in it. The man raised his hand and waved a white cloth.

The lookout waited.

The kayak had sufficient momentum, and when it reached closer to the lookout's boat, he spoke loudly, his hands still raised, 'I have a secret message for the prince.'

The lookout directed another boat and the kayak was escorted to Chung Mung's ship.

Chung Mung was amused at the chicanery of the Ahoms. But he was confident that he would be able to solve the puzzle soon.

He looked down from the main deck of his large ship at the tiny kayak and asked the man in it, 'Yes, who are you? You don't look an Ahom.'

'You are right, prince. I'm one of the Mughal advisors and I have come as the representative of the Mughals.'

Chung Mung frowned and asked, 'Okay. What's your message?'

The man said, 'The Ahoms know about your attack, Prince. You had killed one spy in the jungle. But there was another one, who had made his way back successfully and informed them. Now, the Ahoms are waiting for you at the main gates and—' he pointed towards the walls, 'on the other side of those walls.'

Chung Mung was shocked. But he collected himself in a few moments and responded, 'Thank you for taking a risk to come here and warn me. But how did you learn about this?'

'That's because I was there at the emergency meeting two days ago in the palace.'

Chung Mung smiled, 'Okay, but I still don't get it. What will you get by betraying the Ahoms?'

'Prince, the Mughals want you to win. That's all. Because a weak Ahom empire is not good for us. We want to have a strong army in Jorhat so that we can take its help and expand our empire towards Burma in the east.'

He scratched his chin, 'Makes sense.'

After this, Chung Mung signalled the Mughal advisor to leave.

Now, he was caught in an awkward position. He needed to carefully re-evaluate his plans.

Chung Mung knew that even if the element of surprise was gone, they still were in a stronger position as they had numbers on their side. He thought for a few moments before deciding his next course of action.

Outside their view, taking cover in darkness, Lachit had descended from the wall and entered the river. He was surrounded on all sides by crocodiles. Using sign language, he made a plan with them. Later, he swam back and climbed the wall.

Chung Mung had planned to attack one hour before sunrise. He sent out the forward party. It was a group of twenty small boats with six men in each. The men were wearing black clothes and had coloured their faces with a mixture of black clay and ash. The boats silently reached the base of the wall.

From above, Lachit saw them wriggling against the wall like dark insects. He signalled to his left and right. Twenty stout men were ready on the edge of the wall, holding large urns. These men raised the urns a few inches higher. Now, all they had to do was wait.

A few minutes later, Chung Mung whistled to his men. With this, the men got out their ropes with grapnel anchors and started to climb the wall. The tribals were agile and moved as if gravity had no effect on them.

Lachit watched them. He needed to pick the right moment to act. From the corner of his eye, he saw the remaining flotilla start to approach them.

'Now!' he shouted, just loud enough for his men holding the urns to hear. The men raised the urns together and poured a dark liquid that ran along the walls. This dark liquid was hot oil mixed with sulphur and lime. The result was instant.

The tribals started to slip and fall, crying loudly due to the excruciating pain caused by scalding and blindness. That's when Lachit shot an arrow with a burning tip. Within seconds, the oil on the wall caught fire and the remaining tribals fell back into the water. Only one tribal had managed to climb all the way up and now he stood in front of Lachit and his men, his face frozen due to shock and his body on fire.

On Lachit's signal, a blanket was thrown over him and he was overpowered.

'Take him away. But don't kill him. He's a brave soldier who was fighting a battle he believed in. It's for the court to decide what to do with him. Chung Mung is a savage. We are not.'

The soldiers bowed and carried him away.

Because of the fire, now a portion of the river was visible. Lachit watched Chung Mung through his monocular. The enemy was ordering his fleet to retreat.

Lachit smiled. It was now time for the crocodiles to begin their underwater action.

As Lachit watched, one by one, the boats started to sink. He knew it was the work of the crocodiles who were making holes in the boats' hulls next to their keels, making them flood with riverwater.

The crocodiles succeeded in sinking several boats, but the ships were sturdier and escaped into deeper waters. Many boats managed to flee too.

Jorhat had two walls to protect it from invaders that extended up to six kilometres on either side. Both these walls had gates, which were guarded by Ahom soldiers. But a strip of a hundred metres between the walls was unmanned, as it had the natural protection of a deep-water canal and a stretch of quicksand right next to it.

While the west end of the walls merged with the Brahmaputra, the east end merged with a thickly-wooded area infested with wild animals. The walls, the river and the forest served as natural and man-made barriers, protecting the city for centuries. The only way the enemy could enter the capital, therefore, was by breaching the first gate and then walking on the bridge across the canal and the quicksand to reach the second gate, which they, too, had to overcome.

Meanwhile, at the outer gates, the two other rebel princes, who were Chung Mung's deputies in this battle, had started stage one of their attack by firing several dozen bombs using the four cannons that they had towed to the area. After the Ahom soldiers were successfully pinned down behind the outer gate, they had attacked it with a large number of foot soldiers. The tribal forces were saving the cavalry for the next stage of attack.

Chakradhwaj, who was in command and stationed on top of the inner gates, was glad that the damage to the outer gates and its adjacent walls was not significant in the first wave of attack by the cannons. However, as he observed a large number of tribal soldiers run towards the main gates carrying long poles with them, he was confused. *What's the purpose of these poles*, he thought.

He ordered his archers to fire at them. A sea of arrows was airborne in seconds and Chakradhwaj smiled in anticipation. Nine out of ten of them, he knew, would be killed by their poisoned tips.

That's when tragedy struck the Ahoms. It started to rain. The downpour was so sudden and so heavy that it brought the arrows down before the enemy soldiers could be hit. Now, all he could hear was the sound of thunder and rain.

Outside the outer walls, the rebel tribals stopped for a few seconds but then resumed their approach towards the gates. Within minutes, they forced open the main gates and killed all the Ahom soldiers guarding it. But minutes before the Ahom resistance had died down, in a bid to save their city, the brave soldiers had destroyed the bridge.

Once the tribals had entered the inner space between the two walls, they spread to both sides and began to run with the poles. Now it was clear what the poles were for: they were pole-vaulting across the stretch of water and quicksand. Being agile and athletic, they were able to use the flexibility of their bamboo poles and soon started to land on the ground adjacent to the inner wall.

Here, once again, they pulled out their swords from the scabbards that hung from their waists and attacked the gates of the inner wall.

As soon as the visibility improved, Chakradhwaj observed many tribal soldiers crowding at the main gates. His eyes widened. How was this possible? And then, his eyes fell on the pole-vaulting tribals. It was an unbelievable sight. The rebels had anticipated that the Ahoms would destroy the bridge and had prepared for the contingency. This was clever planning by the rebels.

To control the situation and push the enemy back, Chakradhwaj ordered his archers to fire at the tribals who were crowding near the gate. A rain of arrows targeted them but without much impact. The angle of the Ahom archers was from the top, and the tribals were wearing animal skins on their heads and shoulders for protection, which saved them.

He could hear the wooden doors of the gate creaking as more and more tribal soldiers joined others in pushing it. At this rate, he knew, the gates wouldn't last longer than an hour.

———•———

Back on the riverside, Lachit used a rope to climb down the wall and then dived into the water. A crocodile appeared and he sat on it, cross-legged.

The Ahom ships were anchored nearby. Once he reached the spot, he ordered his crew to set sail. As he stood on the main deck of the largest ship, his flotilla on his sides in an arrowhead formation, the Ahom navy sailed towards Chung Mung's navy. Now that many of the enemy's boats had sunk, the numbers had evened out.

The enemy spotted them and turned. Now, almost fifty ships and boats from each side were on a collision course.

Lachit was trying to spot Chung Mung using his monocular but there was no sign of him. But he knew the rebel prince was very much there directing his flotilla.

As soon as the boats were within firing range, the ships fired cannons at each other, damaging hulls on both sides. A few boats sank. But the two flotillas kept closing in. When the boats came nearer, the soldiers of both sides started to fire arrows.

Around a hundred yards short of the enemy's flotilla, Lachit ordered an alteration of their course to the starboard and then immediately ordered their entire formation to stop. Simultaneously, the ships and boats dropped their anchors. As the anchors ploughed through the soft riverbed, they yawed heavily and shuddered to a stop.

Now, the Ahoms threw ropes with hooks so that they could sling across to the enemy's main boats. On Lachit's orders, they drew their swords, attached their hooks to the ropes and slung themselves to the enemy's boats to fight them in a hand-to-hand battle. Lachit followed them and landed on their main ship.

Although the ship's deck rolled and pitched due to so many people moving and fighting, Lachit felt at home and expertly sliced his hengdang, killing many rebels. Within minutes, the tribals either jumped into the water to save their lives or escaped to the lower decks to hide. Soon, there was no one left to fight. Within a few minutes, the capital ship on which Lachit had earlier sighted Chung Mung had been subdued.

Lachit now climbed onto the monkey island of the ship and shouted from there, 'Chung Mung, show your face and give up.'

His loud voice reached all parts of the ship and a few surrounding vessels too.

Lachit's commanders in other boats also shouted out his challenge, so that his orders could cover the complete area of their naval engagement.

But there was no sign of Chung Mung. That's when Lachit noticed that someone else was ordering the tribals' flotilla from an adjacent ship. This tribal leader was brought in front of Lachit, his hands tied behind him, and pushed onto the deck. He lost his balance and fell down.

Lachit asked him, 'Where is Chung Mung?'

The tribal looked at him. He appeared to be in a daze, but in a split second, his face broke into a smile, showing decaying, betel-nut-stained teeth.

He hissed, 'By now, he must be sitting on the Ahom throne.'

Realizing this was a decoy, Lachit ordered his ships to move towards the main gates at full speed. The trouble was, the river didn't go all the way up to the gates of Jorhat but turned south around six kilometres short. They would have to cover the rest of the journey on foot.

It was eight in the morning, and the wind had picked up. Using the wind in their sails and with well-timed oar movements, Lachit's flotilla reached their intended position fifteen minutes later and ran aground on the riverbank.

The Ahom sailors jumped on the sand and began gearing up for a land attack.

Lachit addressed them, 'Victory to Ahoms!'

Around fifty soldiers shouted back, 'Victory to Ahoms.'

'I want to compliment you for the way you crushed Chung Mung's navy. Each one of you has contributed in this triumph. Now comes the most important phase of the battle. We will charge the main gates and attack the enemy from behind.'

Everyone was listening to their leader wide-eyed, adrenaline coursing through their veins in anticipation of another one-sided armed action.

Lachit added, 'Provided a few of them are still alive. Because I'm confident that, by now, Prince Chakradhwaj and our brave soldiers would have wiped out most of them.'

———•———

A few kilometres from where Lachit was, Chakradhwaj was leading his men from the top of the inner walls, his worries increasing with every passing minute. The tribals were about to break the main gates and he had only one way to stop them.

He sensed a movement towards his left. He turned and bowed. It was Borphukan, decked in full military regalia.

Chakradhwaj said, 'Borphukan, I have got everything under control.'

The Borphukan bent down and, after taking a look at the desperate situation, replied, 'I admire you for your courage, Prince Chakradhwaj. You are like my son, Lachit. But the situation is not under control … why don't you use the wall of water?'

Chakradhwaj said, 'I don't want to do it because the water will weaken the gates even more.'

Borphukan smiled, 'Is there any other way?'

He shook his head.

Borphukan said, 'Do it. We will have a lot of time to repair and strengthen the gates. But we can't allow these brainwashed animals to set foot on our sacred land.'

Chakradhwaj ordered for the water to be released. Within seconds, all the tribals were washed away, but, along with them, a portion of the gate was washed away too. They were safe for the time being but completely vulnerable.

Borphukan asked, 'Where is Lachit?'

Just then, a messenger arrived running and stopped next to them. He said, his voice breaking due to breathlessness, 'Prince Chakradhwaj, Lachit successfully foiled the enemy's attack near the river and he is now approaching the gate from the other side along with his sailors.'

The messenger bowed and left.

Borphukan asked Chakradhwaj, 'What's your plan, Prince?'

'I should go to the enemy before the enemy comes to me and fight alongside Lachit.'

Borphukan smiled and nodded, 'Right. Now go and teach that Chung Mung a lesson. Capture him alive. I want him to be smeared in buffalo dung and paraded around the city.'

Riding on his horse, Chakradhwaj led an army of Ahom's best cavalry and they headed towards Lachit and his sailors.

Borphukan, meanwhile, took over the responsibility of the wall and started to instruct the soldiers on how to repair it.

———•———

Lachit and his sailors had come to a stop. They were still around four kilometres from the gates but the tribal soldiers had surrounded them from all sides.

Lachit looked at them and did an approximate head count. The tribals were around two hundred in number—four times more than them. It was not a comfortable situation to be in. *What was Chakradhwaj doing*, he wondered.

Lachit's sailors and the tribals were eyeing each other. All they needed was an order from their leaders to step forward and start fighting. While Lachit was with his sailors, there was no sign of Chung Mung.

That's when Lachit saw a man on a horse approaching them from a distance, the rising sun behind him. Lachit squinted to confirm if his intuition was right. In a few seconds, as the horse neared, it was clear. The man was Chung Mung.

The tribals started to pound the sand with the end of their spears together, chanting in unison, 'Chung. Mung. Chung Mung …'

Their chorus was deafening and intimidating. Lachit looked at the faces of his sailors closely. The enemy was succeeding in instilling fear in them.

Chung Mung stopped at a distance of around fifty feet from Lachit. He first smiled and then shouted, 'Lachit, my men have surrounded you from all sides. Your end is certain now. There are no crocodiles here to protect you. And your leader, Chakradhwaj, is too scared to step out of the gates. Do you have any last wishes?'

Lachit replied, 'Yes, my last wish today, and always, will remain to lay down my life for the protection of the Ahom kingdom.'

Chung Mung laughed, 'The Ahom kingdom is dead. The honour of the Ahom state, Padmini, is sleeping with the Mughal emperor. And here in Jorhat, the Ahoms now spend their days and nights licking the balls of the Mughal advisors.'

Lachit swallowed his anger. But he knew Chung Mung had every right to say what he was saying. Jayadhwaj had been an incompetent king who lost to the Mughals and whose incompetence ended up dividing the Ahoms.

'Prince Chung Mung, I will not argue about what you are saying. Listen to me; it is still not late. Please accept the fact that we are one. We should fight the Mughals, not quarrel among ourselves.'

'I agree with you, Lachit. Promise me the king's throne and I will unite the kingdom. You have my word. I will also make sure that no harm comes to you or to Chakradhwaj.'

Lachit said, 'Your greed and short-sightedness will cost the Ahom kingdom dearly, Chung Mung. This is not right.'

'Shut up, don't try to teach a prince what is right and what is not. You are nothing but a servant.'

Lachit knew there was no way he could convince Chung Mung to give up. He had learnt nothing from his defeat in the river.

That's when everyone's attention was drawn to the approaching sound of hoofbeats. Chung Mung and Lachit turned their heads in the direction of the sound, but all they could see was a cloud of dust. A large contingent of horsemen was about to reach them. *Who could these be,* wondered Lachit. *Mughal reinforcements? Or more tribals to fight?*

In the next few minutes, Prince Chakradhwaj approached with two hundred horsemen. The needle had now swung in favour of the Ahoms.

Lachit smiled at Chakradhwaj and said to Chung Mung, 'For the final time, I urge you to give up, Prince Chung Mung, while you still have the time.'

In response, Chung Mung ordered his men to attack the combined forces. The tribals attacked them with spears, arrows and swords.

The battle went on for a couple of hours. The tribals fought bravely, but as time progressed, their numbers started to drop.

After a soldier's sword sliced through the leg of Chung Mung's horse, the rebel prince fell to the ground, his sword flying off his hand.

Seeing this, Lachit jumped down from his horse and quickly placed his leg on Chung Mung's wrist so that he couldn't pick up his sword again.

Chakradhwaj reached there too. Chung Mung was now at their feet, trying to crawl away.

Lachit asked, 'What should we do with him, Prince Chakradhwaj?'

'Borphukan wants him alive.'

They tied Chung Mung's hands and legs to a horse and dragged him all the way to the capital's gates.

When they reached the gates, they dumped him before Borphukan. The gate had been repaired and Borphukan had the whole area under control.

Borphukan looked at Prince Chakradhwaj and then Lachit and said, 'Well done, Prince and Lachit.' Then he ordered the soldiers, 'Take this traitor into custody and lock him up in the jail's basement.'

CHAPTER 9

The win over the tribal rebels was celebrated by organizing a special ancestor worship ceremony called Me-Dam-Me-Phi in Jorhat. The priests chanted mantras and the Ahoms thanked the spirits of their ancestors who helped them win.

While the two other rebel princes had died in the battle, Prince Chung Mung's fate was yet to be decided. The tribals had lost many lives, and according to Ahom's intelligence sources, they were now repenting having taken the side of Chung Mung. They also feared that now that Chung Mung had lost, the Ahom soldiers would come to the mountains and ransack their villages. To calm their nerves and to convey the message that the capital had pardoned them, Himabhas sent emissaries to the far-off lands and the mountains where the tribals lived, with the message that there would be no retribution and they should forget about the attack and move on with their lives.

The ancestor worship rituals continued for one week and every Ahom citizen actively participated. When finally, the rituals were over, one morning, Chung Mung was escorted to the court. It was high time that a suitable punishment was given to the traitor according to the law of the land.

As he slowly walked into the court, the shackles hanging from his body clanged disturbingly with every step he took. The expression on his face was completely unreadable.

The Swargadeo's throne was empty, but Himabhas and Borphukan would use the power vested in them to decide the fate of the shackled prince. Besides them, Chakradhwaj, Lachit and other members of the court were present. The guards, as usual, stood on one side. The three Mughal advisors were present too. It was a solemn atmosphere, and all eyes were on the traitor.

After Chung Mung was brought to the designated spot, Himabhas raised his hand, indicating that the proceedings may begin.

Prince Chakradhwaj stood on his feet and began to speak, 'Prince Chung Mung—'

'Just Chung Mung! He doesn't deserve to be called a prince any more,' Borphukan interrupted him.

Chakradhwaj nodded and said, 'Right. Chung Mung instigated the princes of the Ahom kingdom and waged a battle against our land and our people. This is treason, and I recommend a death sentence to be awarded to him.'

There was a pause for a few seconds and then Himabhas said, 'Chung Mung, do you have anything to say in your defence?'

He turned his head to look at those present one by one. The wounds on his body were yet to heal and he sported a few-days-old stubble. He finally grinned and said, 'This court is a joke. You are under the Mughal empire, and it is they who have to decide my fate.'

Chakradhwaj replied, 'Your arrogance is shocking. Honourable Prime Minister, he doesn't deserve a trial. We should have killed him on the battlefield.'

Chung Mung laughed, 'If you had the guts, you would have killed me long ago. But you can't do anything without the approval of your boss in Agra, can you?'

'Enough! Do you have anything to say in your defence or not?' It was Himabhas.

'Yes, I do. The truth is, I didn't instigate anyone. The people of Ahom want to get rid of all of you and they selected me as their leader. The people want a leadership that's courageous and trustworthy, not like Jayadhwaj, who gave his daughter away.'

Borphukan was on his feet, 'Be quiet! We knew about the king's incompetence and tried our best to reform him. What did you or your rebel leaders do? Where were they for the last twenty years?'

Chung Mung stayed quiet.

'All right then, as the prime minister of this court, I—' said Himabhas.

'Wait!' All eyes turned towards Lachit.

Himabhas asked, 'Do you wish to say something, Lachit?'

'Yes, honourable Prime Minister … I was with Chung Mung for six years in gurukul. We have trained together. I know him very well. He's not a bad person. He's made a mistake, but I think he can be reformed. He is not an enemy, even though he did behave like one. He is a prince of our kingdom. I recommend that an exception be made, and he is allowed to live.'

Lachit's unexpected suggestion made everyone think and the court was quiet for a couple of minutes before Himabhas asked, 'Prince Chakradhwaj, what's your opinion?'

'Hmm … The way Lachit has put it … well, I think I would like to second his recommendation.'

'Borphukan?'

Borphukan looked at his son and said, 'The Ahoms only kill during battles. Let's allow this man to repent and reform.'

A count of votes was carried out. The Mughal advisors were invited to vote too.

Most of those present supported Lachit's stand. Chung Mung watched the proceedings as a mute spectator.

Himabhas finally declared the verdict, 'As the prime minster of the Ahom state, and by the powers vested in me by Swargadeo himself, I award a life sentence to Chung Mung.'

There was no reaction of sorrow or relief on Chung Mung's face as the guards took him away, the sound of his shackles ringing throughout the court.

———•———

In Agra, Prince Bahaadur had put a plan in motion that would allow him to meet Padmini and spend time with her without drawing attention. He had got the emperor's approval to take all the royal women for a river cruise on the Yamuna, followed by a royal feast organized on the banks of the river in the shadow of the Taj Mahal.

At seven on an October morning, the queens, princesses and their attendants were brought in chariots to the banks of Yamuna, where six boats waited for them.

The royal ladies were escorted one by one to board the boats. While the chief of the Mughal navy was nominated to be in the first boat to accompany the queens, Princess Padmini was escorted to the sixth boat that Prince Bahaadur had earmarked for himself.

When Prince Bahaadur boarded the boat, his eyes fell on Padmini, and his heart stopped. *How will I gather the confidence to speak to her,* he wondered.

But as she looked up at him, he managed to smile and said, 'Good morning, Princess Padmini. I'm Prince Bahaadur.'

Padmini smiled back, 'Good morning, Prince Bahaadur. It's nice to meet you.'

He kept on smiling, his eyes on her as he stood awkwardly. Padmini's attendants stared at him. The boatmen also stole glances at him from the corner of their eyes.

Padmini felt uncomfortable, and she repeated, 'Prince Bahaadur, it's nice to meet you.'

He understood then and walked past her to occupy the frontmost seat that was reserved for him. He was now seated directly ahead of her.

After a few minutes, the boats started to sail in a single line. The wind was cold but not harsh, and the early morning fog hung heavy on the riverbed like a giant cushion. In the sky, parrots crossed over them and, on both sides of the river, as the boats moved, they saw egrets searching for fish in the shallow patches of the river.

Padmini had noticed Prince Bahaadur earlier too. He had been taking a lot of interest in her and she could sense the attraction he felt for her. Through her sources, she had found out that the prince was among the top three contenders for Aurangzeb's throne. But the emperor was in his mid-fifties and no one knew for how many more years he would maintain his stranglehold on the Mughal kingdom.

In the zenana, there were rumours about the emperor's aggression in the south and the east, and she had overheard people say that he was unhappy to share the power of the Ahom kingdom with the Ahom royalty. He wanted to conquer the state and terminate the existing arrangement.

These rumours had put Padmini in a very precarious position, and her first priority was to warn Lachit. But there was no way she could send a message to him without it being intercepted.

As the boats sailed, sharbat was served to everyone, beginning with the royal women. Seizing the opportunity, Prince Bahaadur turned in his seat and smiled at Padmini. She smiled back.

'I hope you are liking the view, Princess.'

'Yes, I do. You can call me just Padmini, if you wish.'

'Sure … Padmini.'

As the boats sailed over the next couple of hours, Prince Bahaadur described the villages they were crossing, the aquatic birds who were dependent on the river and the variety of fish that was available in its waters. She listened intently though she understood this was merely an excuse for the prince to converse with her.

As Padmini listened to him, an idea started to form in her mind. With that, her smile got wider.

Encouraged, the Prince finally said, 'You are very beautiful Padmini. I love you.'

She giggled, as did her attendants.

By now, they had reached their planned stop. One by one, everyone got down from the boats. The air smelled of skewered meats.

Seating had been arranged for the royal family along the riverbank. Servants went around with trays of dry fruits and meats. A group of musicians played on one side.

Padmini's eyes were searching for the prince. After getting down from the boat, their paths had not crossed. She saw him one moment but lost him in the other due to the movement of people.

By now, it was clear to Padmini that if she played her cards carefully, the prince could become her saviour and the saviour of her kingdom.

Just the prospect made her giddy with excitement. At last, she thought, there was a ray of hope.

That's when her eyes met Bahaadur's for the first time since disembarking from the boat. He smiled, and she matched the width of her smile with his. He started to walk towards her.

When he reached her, he asked, 'Padmini, I hope you are enjoying yourself?'

'It's a beautiful day, Prince. We have a river in Ahom kingdom too. It's called Brahmaputra.'

'Yes, I know.'

'I … I …'

'What is it, Padmini?'

'I'm missing Jorhat today.'

'I'm sorry. My intention in bringing you here was not to make you feel uncomfortable, I just wanted to …'

'All of this was your plan?'

He realized the slip of the tongue, took a deep breath and said, 'Yes, I wanted to spend a day with you and tell you that I love you, and no matter what, I'll always love you.'

She looked away coyly and looked back at him after a few moments. She said, 'I like you too, Prince Bahaadur.'

'Call me Bahaadur, just Bahaadur.'

'Okay.'

The queen came to where they stood and addressed them, 'Look at the two of you. Do you know the gossip that's going around here today?'

'Mother!'

She raised her finger to her lips and whispered, loud enough for both of them to hear, 'Shh … that the prince is in love with Princess Padmini.'

Prince Bahaadur was embarrassed.

Padmini said, 'It's nice to be here with everyone, Queen.'

The queen smiled, 'Let me correct that for you. It's nice to be here with Prince Bahaadur.'

Before Padmini could react, Prince Bahaadur said, 'Mother, enough! Can we spend some time alone?'

'Of course. I didn't know I was intruding.' She laughed and walked away.

The prince said, 'I'm sorry, Padmini. Please don't mind what my mother says.'

'I have no reason to mind, Bahaadur.'

———•———

In Jorhat, Prince Chakradhwaj and Vedha invited Lachit, Borphukan and Yashodhara for a feast at their palace one evening.

By now, a couple of weeks had elapsed since their wedding and Lachit thought of the meal as nothing more than a social obligation. He got ready and came to join his parents. But Yashodhara and Borphukan were not yet ready.

'Father, Mother, we are going to be late.'

Yashodhara said, 'Lachit, we are not royals. What Chakradhwaj is trying to do is against the protocol. We can't go to his palace as invited guests and be treated equal to him and Vedha.'

'Mother, he's my best friend. And he is yet to become the king.'

Borphukan said, 'He's your friend and, so far, you don't have a state portfolio, so *you* can go.'

He raised his hands and tried to convince them. But they had made up their minds.

Finally, Lachit bid them farewell and decided to go alone.

When Lachit arrived at Chakradhwaj's palace, he was received by his best friend right at the entrance with a warm hug and friendly back-slapping. Then he asked, 'Where are your parents, Lachit?'

'They couldn't come. But they have sent their greetings.'

'Kindly thank them when you return.'

Inside, Vedha greeted them.

'Welcome, Lachit,' she said, smiling.

Her expression, body language and greeting were cultured and controlled, and Lachit relaxed.

He replied, 'Thank you for inviting me to your royal home.'

'Let's drink, Lachit,' Prince Chakradhwaj said. 'This is the first time you have come here since our wedding.'

'I'm delighted.'

'We have two things to celebrate—my wedding with my beloved and the win over the rebels.'

They raised their glasses and took a sip.

While the men chatted, Vedha remained in the background, making sure that the snacks and wine were served on time by the servants.

Soon, the two friends seemed relaxed as the alcohol started to soften their edges.

Chakradhwaj was saying, 'You know what, I think we should have killed that bastard Chung Mung. He is a crafty man and his being alive is dangerous.'

'I agree that he's crafty. But we have eaten same food for six years in the gurukul, drank the same water, learnt the same lessons from the same guru.'

'I understand the sentimentality of it, Lachit, but look at what he did to us. Calling him the same as us now will be a grave mistake.'

'I agree! But he can do us no harm by being in the jail. To tell you the truth, he will die a million deaths in prison. It's worse than killing him.'

'Perhaps. I agreed with you, my friend, in the court, because I don't want to go against you, ever.'

Lachit smiled, 'I know. Thank you. And had it not been for you when Chung Mung had surrounded me, he might have overcome us.'

'Until I die, my brother, no harm can come to you.'

'I know, and I'm waiting for the moment when you will become the Swargadeo and sit on the throne.'

'That's what I was trying to tell you. All the other princes who were contenders to the throne have either run away or have been killed. But Chung Mung is still alive and, technically, I can't ascend the throne until he's dead and cremated.'

'He's a traitor, Chakradhwaj. We can convince the court to cancel his candidature.'

'Rumour has it that the Mughal advisors will veto that. They secretly wanted him to ascend the throne. By not killing him on the battlefield, we have complicated matters.'

'Hmm …' Lachit nodded, beginning to understand the seriousness of the problem.

An attendant approached Chakradhwaj and said, 'There's someone to see you, Prince.'

He looked at Lachit and said, 'I'll be back soon.'

After he was gone, Lachit sensed Vedha coming towards him. He looked up.

'Why are you hiding in the shadows, Vedha? You should join us.' He kept his tone friendly and casual.

She said, 'I ... I ...'

Lachit was shocked to see tears brimming in her eyes.

He looked here and there. This was not looking good.

'I suggest you go inside and rest. I'm planning to leave now too.' He got to his feet.

She took a step forward and held his hand, 'No, no. Please don't go.'

Chakradhwaj, who was returning at that moment, saw Lachit and Vedha holding hands. He froze.

Lachit tried to move his hand away but her grip was firm. He couldn't free himself without hurting her.

'Vedha, please leave my hand. You are a married woman.'

'Yes, I'm a married woman, but my soul is not married to him.'

Chakradhwaj cleared his throat and resumed walking towards them.

Vedha dropped Lachit's hand.

Chakradhwaj said, 'Vedha, my beloved, ask the servants to get some more wine.'

Lachit said, 'Chakradhwaj, I would like to leave now. I'm feeling too full.'

'You sure?'

'Yes.'

After this, Lachit nodded at Vedha, hugged Chakradhwaj again and left. Chakradhwaj raised his hand to pat Lachit's back, but he didn't.

After Lachit was gone, Chakradhwaj smiled at Vedha and said, 'Shall we go inside?'

———•———

A few days later, Lachit received a letter from Agra. It was addressed to him by name, but the sender's name was not mentioned. The letter was brought by a special messenger on horseback, who had taken two weeks to reach Jorhat from the Mughal capital.

Who could it be, he wondered, even though a part of him knew who it was. With shaking hands, he opened the envelope using a small knife.

It was a letter from Padmini. He recognized her handwriting instantly. He brought the letter close to his nose and inhaled deeply. He could smell roses.

After kissing the letter multiple times, he started to read it:

My dearest Lachit,

I'm taking a risk by writing this, but it must be done as the future of the Ahom kingdom depends on it. Rumour is rife here that the Mughals will attack Jorhat soon and annex our whole kingdom. After that, they plan to destroy everything that our ancestors have built over centuries: our libraries with all our buranjis, our temples, the Rang Ghar and the palace. We have to start preparing right away and be ready with our full might when they arrive. I pray to Kamakhya Devi that this letter reaches you soon.

One of the emperor's sons, named Muhammed Akbar, called Bahaadur, has started to like me. He says he loves me. His mother approves of the union and if they plan a wedding, I will not be able to do anything. But I want you to know that my soul will always belong to you. Even after I'm married, I will do everything that I can for the honour and safety of the Ahoms.

I miss you every single day, every single hour and every single minute.

I love you,
Padmini

A tear that had rolled from his eye fell on the letter.

He kissed the letter again and reread it. He continued doing this for the rest of the day.

———◆———

The high-security jail where Chung Mung was incarcerated was located in a stone building at the rear of the capital. Heavily guarded by Ahom soldiers, it had three levels: two above ground and one underground. While those under trial were kept on the ground floor, convicted felons were lodged on the top floor and the underground was reserved for the most dangerous criminals.

Chung Mung was lodged in the underground section of the jail. As per the judgement signed by the prime minister, he was kept in a solitary five-by-five-foot room. The tiny room had no bed or a toilet. Chung Mung, who was nearly six feet tall, had to either sleep standing or lie down with his legs folded. Once a week, water was released from one side to clean the room.

The room was always damp as sunlight never reached it and it stank of dead fish, urine and faeces due to lack of ventilation. Next to his room, there were five more rooms like this and, at any given time of day or night, one of the inmates was usually screaming.

Chung Mung had been quiet, trying to conserve his energy. He had factored in this contingency in his overall plans right from the start. He knew, therefore, that as soon he got out of this hellhole, he would kill Chakradhwaj and seize power. His next step would be to kill Lachit, Borphukan, Himabhas, Buragohain and Borgohain, before appointing one of the Mughal advisors as the prime minister and another as the head of the army and the navy.

But the wait had been frustratingly long. Since he was not allowed any visitors, he had no clue what was going on. As more days elapsed, he started to worry. *What if the spies and soldiers loyal to him had turned their backs now that he was in jail? What if they had spilled the beans and disclosed his plans to Chakradhwaj for a few gold coins?* These thoughts made him uncomfortable.

One day, he heard the sound he had been waiting for. Even though he could no longer tell whether it was day or night, he sat up and peered into the darkness.

The sound came again. Yes, it was three hits by a bamboo stick with a one-second interval between them. The code was a confirmation. His rescue plan was underway. He smiled in the darkness, his eyes blinking furiously.

Then, he heard footsteps.

The sounds had woken up other inmates too and one of them started to shout in excitement.

Chung Mung cursed him under his breath and said, 'Shut up and have patience. Help is on the way.'

A fire lamp was lit and it illuminated the underground.

Yes, it was his faithful spy, grinning at him.

Chung Mung said, 'Hurry up.'

The spy opened the iron grill using a key he had brought. Chung Mung stepped out and placed his hand on the spy's shoulders. He said, 'Thank you.'

The other inmates started to plead for their release as well.

Chung Mung turned to face them, grinned and whispered, 'You are enemies of the state. I'm not. So, rot in hell.'

With that, the two of them left, the jailed inmates shouting for help at the top of their voices.

As soon as Chung Mung stepped out, he saw the dead bodies of guards scattered all around.

———•———

Chung Mung reached Chakradhwaj's palace just as he had planned. It was midnight, and the palace was enveloped in darkness. This would be easy, he thought, as Chakradhwaj and his guards would be caught unprepared.

The spy whispered, 'Prince, he has got married and I have heard his wife is very beautiful.'

Chung Mung smiled. 'Yes, I have seen Vedha. Don't worry, I will keep her as a trophy.'

He knew the layout of Chakradhwaj's palace very well. There were four guards at the main gate and another four inside in the veranda.

He looked at the spy and nodded. As they started to move, they were followed by a dozen soldiers waiting a few feet behind them in darkness. Within seconds, trained for this exact purpose, the soldiers swung into action and brought the four guards down without making any sound. Then, they entered the gate and were back in less than a minute after neutralizing the guards inside.

Waiting outside, Chung Mung and the spy had not heard a sound.

'All yours, Swargadeo Chung Mung,' said the spy with a bow.

Chung Mung's chest inflated with pride. The only man now standing between him and the throne of the Ahom kingdom was Prince Chakradhwaj, who was sleeping inside with his newly wedded wife, blissfully unaware that death was standing at his door.

Vedha opened her eyes. She thought she had heard a sound somewhere in the palace. She sat up. Chakradhwaj's side of the bed was empty as he had said he would be returning home late.

She walked towards the open window and stared at the curtains fluttering in the breeze. When she pulled them to one side, she realized that the half-moon was already up. She guessed the time—it was around midnight.

That's when she heard the sound again. This time, it came from right behind her.

Vedha turned around and screamed. There was an intruder standing in front of her. The man jumped on her and placed his hand on her mouth as they fell. He was a big man, his body covered in filth.

She struggled under his weight, but he brought her under control.

Then, he whispered into her ear, 'Where is he?'

She tried to move under him as he repeated, 'Where is your husband?'

He slowly removed his hand.

She opened her mouth, but instead of replying, she screamed, 'Help, help, hel—'

He brought his hand back on her mouth but she bit him this time. As he hurled abuses at her, she managed to free herself and dashed towards the window. He stumbled and fell but was quickly back on his feet again and ran after her.

Vedha was terrified and her survival instincts dictated that she should escape. She had become prey trying to run away from its predator.

Vedha climbed the window and jumped from it, falling down on the wet ground ten feet below. She got up and started to run. Behind her, Chung Mung leapt from the same window and began to follow her.

Chung Mung tried his best to narrow the gap between them but his body was stiff because of the weeks he had spent in jail, where he couldn't even stretch his body.

Soon, Vedha reached the jungle. She kept running; she didn't know where she was going or for how long she would run. She turned to look a few times and her killer was right behind her. She kept running.

Suddenly, she stopped. A huge lion stood in front of her, staring at her. She opened her mouth to shout for help but no words came out. Now, she had predators on both sides.

Behind her, Chung Mung stopped too.

That's when her eyes fell on the lion's feet. There was a carcass of what looked like a freshly-hunted deer. The lion had killed a prey minutes ago. *Would he chase me if I ran*, she thought. Probably not. But she couldn't take a chance.

Chung Mung also noticed the dead deer at the same time. He knew what this meant and he rushed forward to grab Vedha. She started to run again. The lion didn't chase them and got back to his meal.

Now, Chung Mung was just ten feet behind her. She ran as hard as she could. The naked soles of her feet were bleeding now and the flowing garment she was wearing was shredded to bits. Due to the thorny shrubs she crossed, there were scratches on her face and shoulders too.

In the distance, she could see the river. She kept on running.

———•———

Prince Chakradhwaj arrived at the palace five minutes after the attack. He came across the dead guards at the gates and inside the palace compound. That's when a messenger rushed towards him.

The messenger stopped in front of Chakradhwaj and said, 'Chung Mung has escaped from the jail.'

'Where is he?' shouted Chakradhwaj.

The messenger bowed his head, 'No one knows, Prince. Everyone is looking for him.'

Chakradhwaj entered his chamber and didn't find Vedha. That's when his eyes flew towards the open window.

He grabbed his sword and jumped out from it. He started to run towards the jungle.

Ten minutes later, he came across the same lion. He saw a piece of Vedha's garment hanging from a thorny tree towards his left. He changed his direction and continued running.

———•———

The river water was now just a few feet from Vedha and Chung Mung was right behind her. He would reach out at any moment and grab her. Even though she didn't know how to swim, she couldn't stop.

Vedha jumped into the water. At first, she sank and then her head bobbed up, her hands and legs flailing in the water. The current soon pulled her along.

The predator jumped in the water too. She turned and saw him swim towards her. In water, he was faster than her. Vedha kept on splashing, her head in and out of the water, breathing in air and water and coughing.

That's when her head struck something. She turned and there he was—her saviour, Lachit.

Am I dead? Am I hallucinating?

It was by chance that Lachit, who had been missing Padmini after reading the letter she had written to him, had decided to spend some time alone by the river. The emotions he had been feeling were a mix of anger, relief and uncertainty. Given the state of his mind, it wasn't possible for him to get any sleep and he was sitting by the side of the Brahmaputra, contemplating his future course of action once Chakradhwaj became the king and he was appointed the Borphukan. That's when he saw a woman being chased by a man. The woman had jumped into the water and so did Lachit.

Now, he swam with her towards the shore, and once his feet touched the riverbed, he picked her up. The woman was Vedha. Before he could walk through the water, the man who was chasing her hit him from behind. Lachit and Vedha fell in, the water.

Lachit turned and faced his attacker. It was Chung Mung.

Seeing Lachit, Chung Mung's eyes widened. But he controlled his expression quickly, and riding on the hatred he had for Lachit, he plunged forward into the river to attack him. But he had perhaps forgotten that Lachit was now on his favourite terrain.

Lachit dived into the water, emerged behind Chung Mung and hit his head with his hand. Chung Mung groaned and tried to turn his heavy body through water, but Lachit hit him on his neck this time. Chung Mung's eyes rolled back and he fell under the water.

Lachit turned around. Vedha was still bobbing in and out of water. He swam towards her and lifted her. She wasn't breathing, and he quickly stumbled out of the river and placed her on the sandy bank. Then, he started to press her stomach. She coughed and inhaled deeply. He turned her on her side, and more water escaped from her mouth and nose as she took deep gulps of air.

Meanwhile, Chung Mung had stepped out of the water too. He turned to look at Lachit and their eyes met. He started to run away. Lachit chased him.

That's when Chakradhwaj emerged in front of Chung Mung. Now, Chung Mung had Lachit behind him and Chakradhwaj in front of him. He laughed and said, 'At last, I will be able to kill both my enemies at the same time.'

Next to Chung Mung was the sword he had dropped when he jumped into the water. He lifted it up and sliced it through the air, showing his aggression, baring his teeth and shouting unintelligibly.

Lachit shouted towards Chakradhwaj, 'Go and save Vedha. I'll deal with this bastard.'

Chakradhwaj's eyes spotted Vedha fifty feet away from them on the bank. She was trying to sit. He ran towards her as Lachit challenged Chung Mung to come and fight him.

This time, Chung Mung didn't run. He had a sword in his hand while Lachit had nothing, and Chakradhwaj had moved away. The situation had swung in his favour.

He lashed at Lachit. His first strike grazed Lachit's arm. Chung Mung laughed as Lachit cried in pain. Lachit knew that without a weapon, it would be difficult for him to beat the enemy. But he also knew that Chakradhwaj would be by his side any second.

Meanwhile, Chakradhwaj had dropped to his knees next to Vedha. She looked at him through teary eyes and he hugged her.

'Lachit saved me. Lachit saved me.' She repeated.

He kissed her all over her face and hugged her, relieved.

Vedha remained in a trance. She whispered, 'I love you, Lachit …'

With that, she closed her eyes.

Chakradhwaj was shocked. He had his wife in his arms who had just confessed that she was in love with another man. That man had saved her life moments ago. He turned to look at Lachit, who was fighting with Chung Mung and getting beaten. Instead of going to help him, he lay down on the sand next to Vedha and closed his eyes too.

Lachit shouted, 'Chakradhwaj, help me!'

But Prince Chakradhwaj didn't move.

Lachit kept on jumping and moving to avoid getting hit by Chung Mung's sword. Both were getting tired now.

In an instant, Lachit moved forward like lightning and caught the wrist with which Chung Mung held the sword. Then, he punched him with the other hand. Before Chung Mung could recover from the nasty blow that pushed a few teeth back into his mouth, Lachit turned Chung Mung's hand and flipped his own body in such a way that his foot struck Chung Mung's face. A fountain of blood escaped from his mouth and nose. Chung Mung lost his balance and fell, his sword falling from his hands.

Lachit stepped forward and kicked the sword out of his reach. Now, the fight was equal. The two young men fought with their hands, their bodies rolling in the sand. They were bleeding from everywhere. In between, Lachit glanced at Chakradhwaj, who was lying down with his eyes closed.

As time progressed, Lachit's stamina proved to be better than his opponent's. Chung Mung desperately hit out at him but with less and less success, as his legs and hands flailed emptily in the air. He was out of breath, out of energy and out of focus. Lachit danced around him, making sure Chung Mung's punches and kicks did nothing but drain his energy, while he conserved his own.

Finally, when Chung Mung had slowed down enough, Lachit struck his right hand. A bone snapped as his opponent gave a loud cry. Next, Lachit struck Chung Mung's leg with his own. Chung Mung fell on his knees. Lachit leaped over him and, using the power of his punch and his body weight, hit his temple. Chung Mung's eyes closed as he fell on his back.

Lachit sat on his stomach and kept on hitting him till his head was completely buried in the sand. Then, as exhaustion and relief washed over him, he fell on top of him.

A few moments later, Lachit rolled over the enemy and opened his eyes. He heard Vedha's voice in the distance. He got up and ran towards her. She was sitting up and seemed disoriented.

'Vedha,' He called out.

She turned to look at him.

Then Lachit shouted, 'Chakradhwaj!'

Both of them looked at Chakradhwaj, who was still on his back with his eyes closed.

Vedha lifted his head and placed it in her lap. She caressed his face with her fingers and said, 'Chakradhwaj, wake up.'

Lachit watched the tender moment and kept quiet.

Chakradhwaj opened his eyes and he saw his wife's concerned face. He smiled and sat up.

Vedha asked, 'How are you, honey?'

'I'm fine. I'm fine now. How are you feeling?'

She replied, 'I'm fine too.'

He turned to look at Lachit and said, 'Thank you for saving my wife's life, Lachit. I'll never forget this.'

Lachit smiled, 'Come on, that's my duty as your best friend. I think you went into shock.'

Alarmed, Chakradhwaj looked around, 'Where is Chung Mung?'

Lachit pointed towards the body, 'Over there. He's dead.'

'Thank you, Lachit.' His tone was different this time, as if he didn't mean it, Lachit felt. He quickly dismissed the thought.

Something about Chakradhwaj's behaviour was amiss but Lachit couldn't put a finger on it because he had never seen him behave in an odd way before. *Perhaps, I'm overthinking*, he said to himself.

They heard some commotion towards their right as several men emerged through the last line of trees and reached the riverbank. They had swords, spears and bows and arrows in their hands. The soldiers of the Ahom kingdom had arrived.

Chakradhwaj got to his feet, as did Lachit. Then, Chakradhwaj bent down and extended his hand to Vedha. She held it and he pulled her up on her feet.

Chakradhwaj addressed the soldiers, 'We failed at every step and nearly died. I want to investigate this security lapse at the jail and at my palace. The guilty will be punished.'

The soldiers bowed. Then with Chakradhwaj, Vedha and Lachit leading their way, they started to walk back to the capital.

CHAPTER 10

※

Borphukan was at his palace the next morning when one of his armed guards arrived and said, 'A sadhu is here to see you.'

Borphukan looked at Yashodhara, who was sitting with him. He said, 'Bring him in.'

The guard left.

Lachit was still in his chamber, resting. Last night, when he had returned and narrated the attack to his parents, they had listened in horror and finally hugged him in relief.

The Shaiva sadhu walked in. Borphukan and Yashodhara recognized him immediately.

Borphukan asked, 'What do you want?'

It was atypical of Borphukan to treat an ascetic summarily like this, but this time, he was simply following his natural instincts. After all, it was this man who had shaken the confidence of the Swargadeo and foretold the unfortunate future of the Ahom kingdom.

The sadhu stopped next to him while Borphukan remained seated, and said, 'I know you are angry with me, Borphukan. You have every right to be angry. I'm here with a solution that will restore the glory of the Ahom kingdom.'

Yashodhara's expression changed and she stood up. She folded her hands in a belated greeting and said, 'Greetings to you, Sadhu Maharaj. Say whatever you have come here to say and please leave us.'

He smiled and bowed towards her.

The sadhu then looked at the empty chair next to Borphukan and hesitated, as if contemplating if he should sit or not, but didn't in the end. Instead, he said, 'Borphukan, that day, I had overreacted. I'm sorry about the curse I cast on Swargadeo Jayadhwaj. But my purpose is different today.'

Borphukan spoke, his irritation rising, 'Tell us what is on your mind and leave us.'

The sadhu looked around and finally said, 'I want to take Prince Chakradhwaj and Lachit to a sacred place in the mountains. It's the rarest of rare Kamakhya Devi temples. Only a handful of people have gone there so far. If they worship there with pure hearts, the Ahom kingdom will once again become undefeatable.'

Borphukan considered this and he started to yield. In the current situation, their problems were continuing unabated. First, the honour of the Ahom kingdom, in the form of Padmini, had been snatched by their enemies. The second blow was the untimely death of the Swargadeo. The third was the division of loyalty within the Ahom kingdom and the attack by the tribal rebels. Fourthly, there was the escape and attack by Chung Mung. And, finally, that their wealth and prosperity had started to bleed. He knew, once their will to fight hit the nadir, and their coffers ran dry, the Mughals could simply walk in and eat them up.

Perhaps the sadhu was right. At this juncture, Devi Ma was their only hope. The man who stood before them could help them.

———•———

A couple of hours later, Borphukan, Lachit and the Shaiva sadhu were seated in Himabhas's palace when Prince Chakradhwaj arrived.

After greetings were exchanged, Himabhas started to speak, 'The crowning of Prince Chakradhwaj is still two weeks away. Now, the sadhu has brought a proposal that will make the Ahoms undefeatable again. Let's hear his proposal. Sadhu Maharaj, you may begin now.'

The sadhu started to speak, 'My proposal is that the crown prince and the future head of the Ahom army visit the rarest of rare temples of the goddess Kamakhya Devi. This temple is right on top of a mountain. The journey will take a minimum of three days. The path is treacherous, but we must undertake it and pray at this temple to appease our deity. If Prince Chakradhwaj and Lachit undertake this journey and pray at the Devi's feet, her blessings will make the Ahom kingdom powerful again. Once we have the goddess on our side, the Mughals can never defeat us.'

Lachit and Chakradhwaj exchanged glances.

Himabhas asked Borphukan, 'What's your opinion?'

Borphukan replied, 'I'm convinced that this journey is our only hope. That's why I've brought the Sadhu Maharaj here.'

Himabhas nodded and looked at Chakradhwaj.

Prince Chakradhwaj said, 'I'm ready.'

Himabhas looked at Lachit.

Lachit said, 'I'm ready too.'

Himabhas looked at them and said, 'Since all of us are in agreement with this proposal and we are well aware of the power of the sadhu's prophecies, I approve this sacred pilgrimage. Prepare well for it, Prince Chakradhwaj and Lachit, and leave as soon as you can.'

————•————

The next morning, while Lachit's parents bid him farewell, Vedha said goodbye to her husband.

As they started their journey on their horses, the sadhu said, 'I hope your horses will find their way back to Jorhat when we get down and start climbing the steep mountains on foot.'

Both nodded.

By late afternoon, the three of them had crossed the jungle and the river. The mighty Himalayas were now right ahead of them.

The sadhu said, 'This is it. We have to get down and leave our horses here.'

They dismounted, removed their bags and beddings and patted their horses goodbye.

After this, they started to climb the first line of mountains on foot. It was a pleasant and sunny afternoon as the three of them trekked for a couple of hours without stopping.

Just as the sun dipped behind the mountains on the west, the sadhu, who was leading the way, stopped and said, 'We need to halt here for the night.'

They were in a small clearing and the sky towards the west was a deep red and purple. It was the last week of October and winter had almost begun. Out here in the open, they shivered.

Lachit and Chakradhwaj lay down on the ground and looked up. As the dusk dissipated, they realized that they were under a beautiful canopy of a star-studded sky and the trees around them glittered with fireflies.

The sadhu said, 'We need to light a fire to keep the animals away.'

They collected dry twigs and lit a fire. On their way, Chakradhwaj had hunted a rabbit and they cooked it over the live fire. After their meal, Chakradhwaj and Lachit took turns to sleep, the other keeping guard. They didn't disturb the sadhu, who, being at least a couple of decades older than them, needed more rest.

The next morning, they resumed climbing at a steady pace. The sadhu kept up with them without any difficulty. When darkness fell, they once again stopped in a clearing for the night, lit a fire, cooked food and slept.

They woke up the next morning and started their climb again. As the day progressed and they gained altitude, it started to get colder and colder. They were now surrounded by only coniferous trees.

When they stopped in the afternoon for some rest, a few tribals, who lived in the caves in nearby mountains, approached them. The tribals were six in total and all of them carried spears. They wore clothes made of animal hides that had been coarsely stitched together with thin strips of leather.

Lachit and Chakradhwaj wore ordinary clothes to evade recognition but the tribals recognised the sadhu.

One of them asked, 'Man of God, where are you going with these two young men?'

'To Namcha Barwa, at the Devi Mata's temple.'

Their eyes widened.

The second tribal said, 'This is not the right time, man of God. Winter has already set in. These men will freeze to death. Look at them, how they are shivering!'

The first tribal gave them an ointment and said, 'Rub this on your bodies, young men, and it will keep you warm.'

Lachit took the glass bottle that had a dark liquid in it. He shook it and the liquid moved sluggishly, indicating its thick viscosity.

One of the tribals, who had left immediately after greeting the sadhu, returned now. From his hut, he had brought clothes made from animal hides. He offered these to them.

Lachit and Chakradhwaj hesitated. If they accepted them, would they be taking advantage of the generosity of these poor tribals who might be needing these hides themselves, they wondered.

The sadhu solved their conundrum as he said, 'You can take these! These kind people are the children of the mountains and the snow. They live in these very cold parts, but inside their hearts, they have the sunniest of summers.'

Lachit and Chakradhwaj took the clothes, which still had the hollowed-out heads of the animals used to make them attached to them.

While Lachit wore a hide of a bear with the animal's head resting on top of his, he handed over a lion's hide to Chakradhwaj. They looked at one another and laughed. They looked fearsome and funny at the same time.

Later that night, when they stopped again and lit a fire, Lachit told him, 'Chakradhwaj, I received a letter from Padmini a few days back.'

He looked up sharply at him, 'A letter? What did she say?'

'She is fine ... But she said the Mughals are planning to attack Jorhat and annex the Ahom kingdom.'

Chakradhwaj raised his eyebrows, 'But why? We are following the treaty.'

'That's what she said in the letter. And ...' His voice choked.

Chakradhwaj placed a hand on his shoulder and said, 'And what, Lachit?'

'One of the princes would get married to her soon.'

'Oh! I'm sorry.'

Lachit nodded and said, 'Why is God testing me? I have loved only one woman, and he has taken that one woman away from me forever.'

Chakradhwaj said, 'There are other women in Ahom kingdom. You must like someone else too.'

Lachit was shocked, 'What are you saying? You know I only love Padmini.'

Instead of answering, Chakradhwaj closed his eyes and whispered, 'Good night, Lachit.'

Lachit kept on staring at his face for a long time, shocked. He wondered, *how can my best friend go to sleep when I'm talking about the worst crisis of my life?*

The next morning, as they resumed their climb, the sadhu said, 'Now comes the most treacherous part of the journey.'

It had started to snow. He stopped and pointed a finger in one direction and continued, 'Beyond those mountains is the peak of Namcha Barwa. That's where we have to reach.'

Chakradhwaj asked, 'What exactly is there at that temple?'

'There is a sacred lake, and by the banks of the lake is Kamakhya Devi's temple.'

'A lake?'

'Yes, it is a small lake, very sacred. Whoever prays at the goddess's temple with truth in their hearts will get their wishes granted.'

They continued their ascent. But the back-breaking climb had begun to tire them now.

Later at night, when they camped and were shivering uncontrollably, the sadhu said, 'We had crossed the last village this afternoon. Now onwards, we won't find any humans on our path.'

The cold was becoming difficult for the two young men to bear. The sadhu was, however, calm.

The sadhu continued, 'And after tomorrow afternoon, we won't find any animals either.'

Lachit looked at Chakradhwaj and said, 'I think we need more clothes, err … I mean, hides.'

He nodded.

The sadhu said, 'Young men, if you need more clothes, your last chance to kill an animal is tomorrow.'

When they woke up next morning, it was snowing heavily and the visibility was just a few feet. In such a condition, they could neither hunt nor proceed on their journey.

As they waited, uncomfortable with Chakradhwaj's body language since the time they left, Lachit asked him, 'Chakradhwaj, I want to ask you something.'

Without looking at Lachit, he said, 'What is it?'

'You seem to be annoyed with me since we left. Have I made a mistake?'

Chakradhwaj looked at him, his face serious, and said, 'Mistake? If you have made one, you would know, wouldn't you?'

'I know I haven't, but if you feel I have done something, please tell me.'

He stared at Lachit for a long time, his eyes unblinking, and finally said, 'I have nothing to say.'

Then, he looked away. Lachit was not satisfied; there was something on Chakradhwaj's mind but he had no idea what it was. He was sure of one thing, though, whatever was bothering Chakradhwaj would have nothing to do with him. He avowed silently to get to the root of the problem soon and nip it in the bud.

But right now, their problem was nature. Luckily, it had stopped snowing in the afternoon and the weather cleared up. The three of them resumed their climb.

They gave up their search for an animal and, instead, taking advantage of the weather, kept on climbing.

By now, the cold had seeped into their bones.

When they arrived at the summit of Namcha Barwa, it was midday. The sight that welcomed them was surreal. They appeared to be far above the clouds. It was as if they had reached Devlok, the abode of the gods.

Lachit smiled at Chakradhwaj and extended his arms to hug him, 'We made it!'

Chakradhwaj smiled back at him and, ignoring his extended arms, stepped away to marvel at the sight. The sadhu noticed with concern the growing hostility between the two powerful young men, on whom the future of the Ahom kingdom depended.

In the freezing cold, they prayed. By now, Chakradhwaj's hatred for Lachit had reached an all-time high.

While Chakradhwaj prayed that he would kill Lachit soon and place his body under his feet during his coronation, Lachit prayed for Padmini's freedom and the safety of the Ahom kingdom from the Mughals as he pictured himself as a shield, with Chakradhwaj's feet on his shoulders.

There was a huge roar of thunder in the sky. It was clear, the two most powerful men of the 600-year-old Ahom kingdom were enemies now. The sadhu sensed this and his eyes grew wide with terror.

GLOSSARY

1. **Swargadeo**: The kings of the Ahom kingdom of modern-day Assam, who were essentially Tai people, were addressed as Swargadeo. According to some historians, the Ahom kings were considered to be reincarnations of Lord Indra, the god of heaven, and were therefore called Swargadeo.

2. **Ahom kingdom**: From 1228 to 1826, the region that is called Assam today was ruled uninterrupted for almost six centuries by the Ahom kings. The first Ahom king was a Tai prince called Sukaphaa who had crossed the Patkai mountains from Mong Mao in the east and arrived in the Brahmaputra valley with 9,000 soldiers. By the time of his arrival, the Kamarupa kingdom had declined, and there were many minor tribal chiefs controlling different parts of the valley. Sukaphaa

brought with him the knowledge of wet rice agriculture, which was until then unknown to the people of the area. Over time, with diplomacy, he established the Ahom kingdom, which subsequent kings expanded by assimilating the local tribals.

3. **Gamosa**: A multipurpose rectangular piece of cloth used from ancient times in Assam. Its uses range from wiping the body and wearing it on the head to serving as a gift during ceremonial occasions, as a covering for the altar or for placing sacred scriptures on it. A gamosa typically has a red border on the sides and motifs printed or embroidered on its ends.

4. **Tongali**: A gamosa, when tied on the waist over a shirt, is called a tongali.

5. **Safa**: A headgear typically worn by men of royal lineage in the Ahom kingdom. It was usually made of silk and wrapped around the head with or without gold ornaments as embellishments.

6. **Luk-Lao**: Undiluted rice wine that was consumed by the Ahom people.

7. **Borphukan**: Borbarua and Borphukan were two military commander positions of the Ahom kingdom, reporting directly to the king. They were also the heads of the judiciary.

8. **Dangarias**: Dangarias were the two Gohains, Buragohain and Borgohain, who were independent kings under the overall rule of the Swargadeo of the Ahom kingdom. They were the direct descendants

of the first Ahom king Supakhaa who had vowed not to lay a claim to the Swargadeo's throne of the Ahom kingdom.

9. **Patra mantris**: The five council ministers under the Swargadeo were the patra mantris and the eldest among them was designated as the raj mantri or the prime minister.

10. **Shaiva sadhu**: A Hindu ascetic who is a follower of Lord Shiva and typically wears three horizontal ash lines on the forehead with a red mark at the centre of the middle line.

11. **Rudraksha**: Rudrakshas are prayer beads used by Hindus, Jains and Sikhs. They are traditionally made of stones of non-edible fruits from trees belonging to the genus *Elaeocarpus*, which is native to India, Nepal, Sri Lanka, Indonesia, northern Australia, etc. For the followers of Lord Shiva, the use of rudraksha is particularly sacred.

12. **Langot**: A triangular loincloth worn by men of the Indian subcontinent.

13. **Gunwale**: The top edge of the sides of a boat is called the gunwale.

14. **Hengdang**: The hengdang was a long-handled single-edged sword used by the Ahoms in India. The handle was made of wood, gold or silver, depending on the person's position in the Ahom hierarchy.

15. **Damaru**: A small two-sided drum with a narrow waist from where it is held and shaken so that the beaded

strings attached to both faces of the drum can hit the membrane and make rhythmic sounds. In Hinduism, the damaru is synonymous with Lord Shiva and is used by devotees while praying or conducting Shaiva ceremonies. It is also used for meditation purposes by Tibetan Buddhists.

16. **Paik**: All men between sixteen and fifty years of age in the Ahom kingdom, who were not of royal lineage, from the priestly caste or a slave, were known as paiks. Each paik had to serve for three months in the Ahom army every year, for which he was duly paid from the royal treasury. For the rest of the year, he could work in his fields and was not paid. A Bora commanded 20 paiks, a Saikia, 100 and a Hazarika, 1,000. Similarly, a Barua commanded 3,000 paiks and a Phukan, 6,000.

17. **Naubaicha phukan:** The admiral of the Ahom fleet of ships and boats.

18. **Kopou ful**: The state flower of Assam and Arunachal Pradesh, its common English name is foxtail orchid. The flower is also grown in Odisha, Andhra Pradesh (where it is called chintaranamu by the locals) and West Bengal, besides Thailand, Cambodia, Sri Lanka, China, Bhutan, Myanmar, Indonesia, etc. In Assam, it is used during festivals and celebrations as a symbol of love, happiness and victory.

19. **Karambhumi**: In the context of an individual, it means the purity and honesty of a man's actions that makes him successful.

20. **Shishya**: In Hinduism and Buddhism, a disciple who is learning under a guru or a teacher is called a shishya.

21. **Sanchi**: Buranjis, or the official records of Ahom Kingdom, and other books, were written on the barks of the sanchi (Aquilaria) tree or aloe wood.

22. **Rang Ghar**: Located adjacent to the palace of the Ahom kings, the Rang Ghar was a royal sports pavilion where buffalo fights, races and major festivals like Rongali Bihu were conducted and witnessed by royal families, the nobility and the masses.

23. **Pepa**: Pepa is a wind musical instrument made from a hollowed-out buffalo's horn that is attached to a reed with holes on it for blowing air so that sound and pitch can be controlled by the person playing it.

24. **Suti sula**: A short shirt worn by the Ahom kings and common subjects. Depending on the hierarchy, it could be made of silk or cotton.

25. **Suria**: Clothes worn by Ahom men below their waist. Depending on the hierarchy, just like suti sula, it could be made of silk or cotton.

26. **Mekhela chador**: It is a two-piece traditional dress worn by Assamese women. The lower part, called mekhela, is wrapped below the waist, and the upper part, called chador, is loosely draped over the upper body with one end tucked into the mekhela. A traditional blouse when worn under the chador is called a riha.

27. **Yagna**: An ancient Hindu ritual practice in which Vedic hymns are chanted by the devotees in front of a fire.

28. **Xorai:** A container manufactured from bell metal which has a tray and a stand. It was used by the Ahoms to offer gifts to priests and important guests and is used to this day in Assam for ceremonial purposes.

29. **Tamulpan:** The areca nut and betel leaves offered to special guests. The ceremonious gifting of the tamulpan symbolizes friendship, respect and devotion.

30. **Knuckle bow:** The protective cover around the handle of a sword that could be made of metal or leather is called a knuckle bow. Its purpose is to protect the fingers and the knuckles of the user's hand.

31. **Sowar:** Drawn from the Hindi–Persian word sawar, which means 'to ride', sowar was the rank of a cavalryman in the Mughal army.

32. **Vaid:** A medical practitioner, typically from India and Nepal, who prescribes Ayurvedic medicines to treat diseases.

33. **Zenana:** In South Asia and in Iran, the part of a large house or a palace that's secluded for accommodating the women is called a zenana. It is usually guarded by female guards and eunuchs, and men are not allowed to step inside.

34. **Chak-long:** The traditional wedding ceremony of the Ahoms that lasts for nine days is called chak-long. Nowadays, the ceremony is mostly conducted over three days.

35. **Pani-tola:** One of the wedding rituals of the Ahom people in which women visit the river early in the

morning to fetch freshwater, which is then used to give a bath to the bride and the bridegroom while the women sing and dance.

36. **Kavac-kapor**: A piece of clothing made by the bride in a single night, right from weaving cotton threads for making the fabric to stitching and making a garment out of it. The gesture is meant to symbolize that this cloth made by the bride will protect the bridegroom.

37. **Muga silk**: A variety of wild silk that's geotagged to the state of Assam and is known for its lustre and durability. Naturally golden in colour, it has been used by the royalty and rich people of the Brahmaputra valley since time immemorial.

38. **Barman Kachari**: The Barman Kachari is a Scheduled Tribe community that ruled parts of modern-day Assam and Arunachal Pradesh in the fourteenth and fifteenth centuries and fought many battles against the Ahoms until the latter defeated them and sacked their capital. The people belonging to this community are now scattered all over Northeast India. Their language is Tibeto-Burman, which is considered a highly endangered language spoken by only a handful of native speakers, most of whom are old.

39. **Chutias**: The Chutia kingdom (pronounced Sutiya or Sadiya) was a small independent country located on the north of the Brahmaputra River in modern-day Assam and Arunachal Pradesh from 1187 until 1673, when it was defeated and absorbed into the Ahom kingdom.

40. **Monkey island**: A deck located directly above the navigating bridge or wheelhouse of the ship. It is the topmost accessible location of a sailing ship that's often used as a lookout.

41. **Ancestor worship (Me-Dam-Me-Phi)**: A communal worship of ancestors by the Ahoms that was celebrated on 31 January every year. It was also conducted to commemorate a military win. 'Me' means offerings, 'Dam' means ancestors and 'Phi' means gods.

42. **Buranji**: The official records of activities of the Ahom state written and maintained on the orders of the king. This tradition was started by the first king and continued till the last one. Brevity was the essence while writing these records. Unofficial buranjis were also written to record and document the activities of certain families or regions. Buranjis were written on the barks of sanchi trees.

43. **Grapnel anchor**: A kind of anchor, primarily used by smaller ships, which is lightweight and has around three to six hooks or flukes. When tossed in the water, due to its multiple hooks, it can get hold of almost anything.

44. **Sharbat**: A sweet drink of Iranian origin that historians believe was brought to the Indian subcontinent by the Mughals. Today, it is usually made by mixing concentrated or dried fruit powder with sugar and water. With numerous regional variations in use now,

it is a popular non-alcoholic drink consumed in many parts of Asia and Europe.

45. **Namcha Barwa**: It is a peak (7,782 metres above mean sea level) which is located, as the crow flies, approximately 60 kilometres north from Arunachal Pradesh's border in Tibet. Only a handful of people have scaled its peak.

ABOUT THE AUTHORS

Vijayendra Prasad is an Indian screenwriter and film director who has worked in Telugu, Tamil and Hindi cinema for more than four decades. A screenwriter for more than twenty-five films, most of his movies have been blockbusters that have set new records at the box office. A few of his most popular films include *Baahubali: The Beginning, Baahubali 2: The Conclusion, RRR, Manikarnika: The Queen of Jhansi, Bajrangi Bhaijaan,* etc. In 2016, he won the Filmfare Award for the Best Story for the film *Bajrangi Bhaijaan.* Vijayendra Prasad has directed films too, and in 2011, for his Telugu film *Rajanna,* he won the Nandi Award for the Best Feature Film. Since July 2022, Vijayendra Prasad is a nominated Member of Parliament (MP) to Rajya Sabha.

A product of the Naval Officers' Academy, **Kulpreet Yadav** has spent two decades as an officer in uniform and has successfully commanded three ships in his career. Since his retirement as Commandant from the Indian Coast Guard in 2014, he has authored several books in diverse genres, including espionage, true crime and military history. Winner of the Best Fiction Author Award for *Murder in Paharganj*, an espionage novel, at the Gurgaon Literary Festival in 2018, Kulpreet is also an actor and screenwriter. He lives in Mumbai, and his latest book is *The Battle of Rezang La* (Penguin, 2021).

30 Years *of*

 HarperCollins *Publishers* India

At HarperCollins, we believe in telling the best stories and finding the widest possible readership for our books in every format possible. We started publishing 30 years ago; a great deal has changed since then, but what has remained constant is the passion with which our authors write their books, the love with which readers receive them, and the sheer joy and excitement that we as publishers feel in being a part of the publishing process.

Over the years, we've had the pleasure of publishing some of the finest writing from the subcontinent and around the world, and some of the biggest bestsellers in India's publishing history. Our books and authors have won a phenomenal range of awards, and we ourselves have been named Publisher of the Year the greatest number of times. But nothing has meant more to us than the fact that millions of people have read the books we published, and somewhere, a book of ours might have made a difference.

As we step into our fourth decade, we go back to that one word – a word which has been a driving force for us all these years.

Read.

Harper
Collins

HARPER
PERENNIAL

HARPER
BUSINESS

HARPER
BLACK

हार्पर
हिन्दी

HarperCollins
Children'sBooks

HARPER
DESIGN

HARPER
VANTAGE

Harper
Sport